Falling For Autumn

Book Two in the Music City series

Joan Wahl

Copyright

Ebook: 978-1-966625-06-3
Paperback: 978-1-966625-07-0

Published by Defiance Press & Publishing, LLC
Bulk orders of this book may be obtained by contacting Defiance Press & Publishing, LLC. www.defiancepress.com.
Defiance Press & Publishing, LLC
281-581-9300
info@defiancepress.com

Dedication

Writing a novel is not a solo effort. Mine would not be in your hands (or on your device) without all the people who encouraged me along the way.

To my husband, Roger, who taught me the true meaning of love.

To my daughter, Carolyn, who fills my life with joy, and taught me to never give up.

To my three biggest cheerleaders – Susie, Cammy and Luella. Thank you for your unwavering enthusiasm!

To my favorite independent bookstore, Werner Books, for supporting me and introducing me to other local authors.

And last, but certainly not least, my publishing team. Mark, Kelly and Lisa, you took my dreams, polished them up, and turned them into reality. I can never thank you enough.

Chapter One

'**I**s your sister married to Martin Brody?'

Autumn realized it should have come as no surprise to her that her twin being married to someone famous would affect her ability to find love. She'd tried everything, including agreeing to several blind dates set up by well-meaning friends and even putting her profile on a dating site. But it seemed to her that each encounter either began or ended the same way, with the same question.

She and Greg were on their third date, and she thought it looked promising up to the point when he handed her a demo disk and asked her to pass it along to Martin. She walked out of the restaurant and left it on the table.

The next day, after an early dismissal, Autumn replayed last night's turn of events to one of her coworkers, Betsy Danielson.

Betsy commiserated with her and then offered up the crazy suggestion that Autumn should apply to be a contestant on *The Bachelor* .

Autumn couldn't quite wrap her head around the idea of competing with 20 or more women for the heart of one man.

"I enjoy watching it, but it all seems so … unrealistic. Especially when they start talking about how quickly they develop feelings for someone they met a few weeks ago."

Betsy was happily married and offered to set Autumn up with her husband's brother, Aaron.

"Trust me when I say he probably has no idea who your brother-in-law is, much less that he is married to your sister."

"How can someone live in the greater Nashville area and not know who he is?"

"He's a recent transplant from Chicago. Divorced, with one daughter who lives with her mother."

"Recent divorce? I don't want to be the rebound."

"They've been divorced for a couple of years now and seem to co-parent without a lot of animosity. I've never heard him say a bad thing about her."

That was a huge plus in Autumn's mind. She had students whose parents used them like bargaining chips.

"What brought him to Tennessee from Chicago?"

"Work. He's a project manager for a large architectural firm. Travels a lot. He's having a hard time meeting someone too. Although for different reasons, obviously. Do you want me to try to set something up?"

"Give me a few days to think about it."

Betsy headed for home, when Autumn suddenly realized someone else had come into the teacher's lounge.

"Autumn?" Tom Williams startled her. "Sorry – I didn't mean to eavesdrop."

She waved a hand as if to say it didn't matter. "Don't worry about it, Tom. If I'd wanted to have a more private conversation with Betsy, I would have done it someplace else."

"Well, it's just that I have an idea."

Tom seemed like a nice enough guy, slightly younger and reasonably attractive, but she did not want to date someone she worked with. Before she could voice that, he continued.

"A friend of mine and I went to a speed dating event last month at O'Reilly's. It was kind of fun. They have it once a month, and the next one is in a few days. If you're interested, you could call and see if they still have any openings. They obviously have to have the same number of men and women at each event."

Autumn felt skeptical, but then again, why not? Nothing else had worked.

"Did you meet anyone you wanted to try to get to know a little better? Or did it feel more like a waste of time?"

"Both Jack and I thought we had a bit of a spark with someone. But it was just our luck that we both felt it with the same woman."

"That must have been awkward."

"It could have been, but we both decided it wasn't worth one of us pursuing her. Jack and I have been friends since middle school, so we decided to go to the next one."

Autumn decided to give it a try, and when she called O'Reilly's, they informed her they had one spot left for a woman. She thought it seemed like a sign.

When she arrived two days later and signed in, she was surprised at how many people were there. Some men appeared to be a bit older than she was, but she also knew they had age limits each night, so none of them would be more than 5 years younger and no more than 10 years older than her. She had no issues with dating an older man. Recent experience had taught her that men her own age were not as mature, on average. But she also didn't rule out the possibility of dating a slightly younger man.

She had spent the last few days thinking about what she would say about herself in the four-minute time limit, but hadn't really come up with anything she thought would set her apart from the crowd. She could have asked Summer or one of her friends for suggestions, but she didn't want them to try to talk her out of it.

They were about to start when a latecomer arrived, and they hurried to get him signed in. Their eyes met across the crowded room, and it was suddenly hard for her to breathe. His intense gaze seemed to land directly on her, even though a couple of dozen people separated them. Unfortunately, based on his late arrival and seat assignment, he would be the last one she met.

When things got started, she was still feeling nervous and wasn't even quite sure what she said to the first few men. She was normally very confident, but she tried to chalk it up to how both quickly and slowly things seemed to be going at the same time.

Autumn tried to be present for each encounter, but all she could think about was that every four minutes, she was one chair closer to the only man in the room who had managed to capture her attention, without a single word spoken between them.

Suddenly, when only five chairs separated them, the power went out. Emergency lights came on, but everything else stayed off, including the computer system and cash registers.

The owner announced that a large percentage of the other businesses on the street were also dark, so they had no choice except to end the evening.

Autumn wondered about the rules. Could she simply walk up and introduce herself? Ask for his name? She considered doing just that when Tom and Jack approached her. When she explained that there was someone she wanted to meet but hadn't had the chance to, they encouraged her to go talk to him. She tried to make her way through the crowd when she saw him take a phone call and leave.

The following day, she stopped at O'Reilly's after work and became frustrated by her inability to find out anything about him. She knew where he had been sitting when the power went out and what he had been wearing, but she wasn't getting anywhere.

The assistant manager, Janice, explained, "We can't give out anyone's personal information. It's one thing to exchange numbers after the event is over. But you're telling me you didn't even get to talk to him?" Janice looked very dubious.

"Okay then, how about this? I'll leave you my name and my phone number. If someone comes in wanting to find me, you can pass it along."

Now Janice looked even more skeptical. "To anyone? Everyone? We've already received a few calls about this. I'll tell you the same thing I told everyone else. We know what everyone's seat assignments were. We will rearrange them so everyone gets to meet the rest of the men and women. That's the best I can do."

Autumn agreed to return the following week, but in the meantime, she had already agreed to a double date with Betsy, her husband Dan, and his brother, Aaron. She convinced herself it seemed silly to hold onto the hope that she and the man from O'Reilly's would hit it off.

She met everyone at the restaurant and had an unexpectedly nice time. Aaron was handsome, well-spoken, and a gentleman. He didn't monopolize the conversation and seemed genuinely interested in getting to know her. The only obvious drawback was that he moved frequently for work, and even though she loved to travel, that did not appeal to her. She spent a lot of time with her family, particularly Summer and Brody and their twins, Leo, and Lucia. She wanted to be around to watch her niece and nephew grow up.

They left the restaurant together, and Aaron walked her to her car. If they had left only seconds later, she would have come face-to-face with the man she so desperately wanted to find.

As he approached the restaurant, he recognized her laugh. He watched her walk away, the setting sun turning her hair the color of shimmering gold with strands of red. All he could think was that he had found her too late, wishing he could be the man by her side.

Autumn waited, not so patiently, for the rescheduled speed dating event. This time, she took a little more care with her appearance. She confessed to Betsy what she had done and asked for her help picking out an outfit. Autumn tended to downplay her curves, but Betsy convinced her she should display them in a tasteful manner instead.

Autumn loved her twin dearly and didn't have a jealous bone in her body, but she had always thought Summer was the beauty in the family. Autumn's hair was unruly but admittedly a beautiful color of reddish gold. She thought of that as her best attribute, and Betsy convinced her to leave it down.

She arrived at O'Reilly's with time to spare and looked around the room for the one man she most wanted to meet. She took her assigned seat and counted two fewer people than had been at the last event.

Janice took the microphone and said, "Before we begin, I would like to point out that there is one less man and one less woman here. They each dropped out. I can only conclude that they made a connection last week and did not feel the need to return. However, I can assure the rest of you that you will get to meet everyone else this evening."

Autumn found it hard to hide her disappointment but she stayed anyway, even though her heart wasn't in it. She knew she wasn't giving anyone a fair chance, and she just wanted the evening to end. She managed to sneak out before Tom and Jack could corner her to ask her about the mystery man.

She went home, feeling unsettled and upset. It wasn't like her to feel instantly attracted to someone. She had never experienced that lightning bolt of attraction that Summer and Brody had felt the first time they looked in each other's eyes. Until now.

Chapter Two

She thought about stopping to see Summer but decided that the morning would be soon enough. When she and Dallas ended their engagement, she moved into an apartment in the same complex where Summer lived. After Summer and Brody got married, they offered to let her live in the guest cottage on their property rent-free. After the twins were born Autumn liked to tease them that they wanted her there for the free babysitting, but in reality, the proximity worked out well for everyone. Summer's marriage to Brody and the arrival of the twins had not altered the closeness Autumn and Summer enjoyed.

Autumn arrived at the main house the following morning to an unfamiliar set of twins with energy and loud voices. Summer and Brody's twins, Leo, and Lucia, had just turned three. Surely they were still too young for playdates?

Her usually unflappable sister looked like she hadn't slept for a week. "Who are these little hellions?" Autumn raised her voice in order to be heard.

"Sam and Alex. They've only been here for a few hours and I'm pregnant and—"

"Wait a minute! Back up!"

"They've only been here for a few hours and—"

"You're pregnant?"

This was not the way Summer wanted to share the news. "Sorry. That just sort of slipped out. We just found out this morning." Summer started to turn a little green and rushed to the nearest bathroom.

When she returned, Autumn made her sit down and went to get her some crackers and ginger ale. But as she walked towards the kitchen her steps faltered. She tried to convince herself she was imagining things, having only heard his voice briefly the evening of the first spend dating event. Not only that, but why would he be here of all places? Her curiosity got the better of her and she opened the kitchen door to discover Brody sitting next to an unfamiliar man. But he wasn't just *a* man. He was *the* man. They were so deep in conversation that neither one of them noticed her.

"Brody, I need a wife. I can't believe Julia's parents want to take custody of Sam and Alex. I also can't believe that they still blame me for Benjamin's death and Julia's cancer."

Autumn struggled to try to follow their conversation. His voice matched the concern in his tired eyes. He was obviously distraught and rambling, but she was intrigued.

"Spencer, you can't just up and marry someone to try to keep your family together. Julia's parents would see right through that, and you would be worse off than you are now."

"That's why it needs to be someone you know. I'm not talking about a real marriage; I'm talking about the appearance of one. Someone you could have introduced me to."

"I'll do it." The words rushed out of Autumn's mouth before she could stop them.

When Spencer finally turned to look at her, he grasped the kitchen counter to steady himself.

"It's… you," he finally managed to get out. "I didn't think I'd ever see you again."

Brody turned around so fast he almost slipped off the kitchen stool.

"Autumn—how much did you hear? And, correct me if I'm wrong, but do you two know each other?"

Autumn and Spencer only had eyes for each other.

"I tried to find you," Autumn admitted, "but no one would give me your contact information. And then you didn't return for the second night."

"I saw you—leaving a restaurant with someone. Someone I assumed you met at the speed dating event."

Hope shone brightly in Autumn's eyes and her voice even though she tried to remain calm.

"Was that why you didn't come back?"

"I know this is going to sound crazy..." Spencer trailed off, not wanting to scare her off.

"Try me."

"When I looked across the room at you, I just felt... something. Like we were both there for a reason. Not to meet someone. To meet each other."

Brody watched the two of them with a feeling of nostalgia. Was it possible his wife's twin experienced the same kind of unreal, undeniable chemistry with Spencer that he had felt the first time he looked in Summer's eyes?

Summer walked into the kitchen and experienced her own sense of déjà vu. Why were her sister and Spencer looking at each other like they had just found the missing piece of their heart puzzle?

"What's going on?"

"Autumn agreed to marry me," Spencer responded so matter-of-factly you would have thought he simply announced they were out of coffee.

"Autumn? Fill me in here," Summer demanded, playing the big sister card even though she was less than ten minutes older than her twin.

Autumn desperately wished she had already filled Summer in on the whole speed dating experience so she wouldn't question the reasons behind Autumn's offer to marry a man she barely knew. Even Autumn could admit it was a crazy idea. So why did it feel so … *right* ?

"The only men in my life want to date me so I will introduce them to Brody. I'm hoping time might change that. How long were you thinking we'd have to stay married? Two years? Five?" She stopped to take a breath. "I assume this would be a marriage in name only?"

"I was thinking three years."

She noticed he refrained from answering her other question, and she wondered for a moment if he planned – or hoped – that they would share a bed. Maybe she wasn't the only one who felt the chemistry crackling in the air.

"We'll need to come up with a script. Where and when did we meet? How can we explain you never introducing me to your children?" Autumn inquired.

"Naturally, I would have wanted to wait to introduce you to them until we knew we wanted to make a commitment."

"He needs a wife so his former in-laws can't get custody of his children," Autumn informed her sister.

Summer was astounded and more than a little apprehensive. Brody trusted Spencer, but she barely knew him. "In this day and age? That hardly seems likely."

Spencer threaded his hands through his dark hair, already showing strands of gray by his temple. "It's a much longer story than that."

Summer pulled up a chair and sat down. "Grace is coloring with the kids. Enlighten me."

"Who's Grace?" Autumn inquired.

"My twelve-year-old daughter."

"Any more stepchildren I should be aware of before we say I do?"

"You two are crazy," Brody commented, finally putting in his two cents.

Spencer began to give them the background so they would know the basis for his fears. "Julia was my college sweetheart. We got married when I graduated from law school. A few years later, our son, Benjamin, was born, and two years after that, we had Grace. Julia had a difficult pregnancy with Grace, and her doctor cautioned us against having more children. She wasn't as accepting of that as I was, but we already had two healthy children. I told myself she would come around, and I made peace with that until…." His voice started to tremble with emotion.

Autumn reached out to cover his hand with hers, and the spark nearly rendered her speechless and made it nearly impossible to concentrate on anything except him.

"Until?" was all she managed to ask.

"Ben went to camp. Grace was supposed to go too, but she came down with chicken pox. One night, he and two other boys snuck out of their cabin and went down to the lake. They took a canoe out, and…. Ben didn't have on a life jacket. It was a stupid mistake that cost him his life. The other boys tried to save him. They finally went to get help. By the time they found Ben's body, it was too late." His eyes shimmered with unshed tears.

"How awful," Autumn said quietly, trying to hold back tears of her own.

Once Spencer regained a small measure of control, he continued. "Three years later, my wife came home from work one day and announced she was pregnant. We hadn't talked about having more children, and I couldn't believe we weren't on the same page. I was initially furious, and I am ashamed to admit I didn't handle it well. She said she would give me a week to come to my senses, and she took Grace and went to stay with her parents."

"But surely she realized you were worried about her health," Autumn offered. "Because otherwise I'm assuming you would have been thrilled?"

Spencer nodded. "She came home after only 48 hours, but the damage was already done when it came to my relationship with her parents. It recovered somewhat when we discovered she was carrying twins. The pregnancy went better than expected, and Sam and Alex were both healthy. But Julia never really recovered from their birth, and a few months later she was diagnosed with a rare form of ovarian cancer. Which, as her doctor explained it, had progressed too rapidly to treat. So, just about the time her parents and I had gotten back on somewhat even footing, their daughter died."

This was the saddest story Autumn had ever heard, and trying to hold back her tears would have been like trying to stop the flow of water over Niagara Falls. "Your wife died. And they tried to blame you?"

His gray eyes turned the color of a turbulent sea. "It was my fault. I should have gotten a vasectomy."

"Did you suspect she was trying to get pregnant?" Brody asked.

"No," Spencer admitted, "but that doesn't mean I shouldn't have done anything and everything in my power to protect her."

Chapter Three

J ust then, the kitchen door flew open, and four little balls of energy came running in, followed by someone whom Autumn assumed must be Grace.

Autumn studied Spencer's daughter, who looked far too sad and solemn for a twelve-year-old. Was she trying to fill the role of mother to her young siblings?

Grace went to stand next to her father, and Autumn noticed that they had the same unusual eyes. They reminded her of a gray December sky right before a snowstorm.

"I think it's past nap time for all of them." Brody announced, hoping his wife might also agree to take a nap.

Summer and Brody stood and ushered Leo, Lucia, Sam, and Alex out of the kitchen.

Once they were gone, Spencer and Grace turned their identical gazes toward Autumn, and she felt a bit like a bug under a microscope.

Autumn reached out a hand to Grace. "I'm Autumn, Summer's twin."

"I like your name," Grace replied shyly.

"Are you curious about why she is named Summer and I am named Autumn?"

Spencer and Grace both nodded, although Spencer thought he had heard the story from Brody.

"Well, even though we are twins, we don't share the same birthday. Summer was born just before midnight on the last day of summer, and I was born just after midnight on the first day of fall."

"Cool," Grace responded with enthusiasm. "So, you could each have your own birthday parties." She turned to face her father. "We better not tell Sam and Alex that story, or they will each want their own party."

Spencer smiled sadly and ruffled her hair. "You're right. Best we keep that to ourselves."

As hard as Spencer had tried to keep Grace in the dark about what her grandparents were planning, he soon found out how wrong he was.

Grace turned toward Autumn with curiosity. "Are you the one?"

"The one what?" Autumn stammered.

"The one my father is going to marry so my grandparents can't take Sam and Alex?"

Autumn and Spencer were both struck speechless, but he recovered first.

"What do you know about that?"

"I know they want them, but they don't want me. I was only eight when my brother died. Do they blame me for not going to camp?" Grace backed up very suddenly, as though something dreadful just occurred to her. "Do you blame me?" she asked in a soft, tear-filled voice.

How, Spencer wondered, was it possible that they had never talked about this? In the years since the accident, had he been so grief-stricken that he just couldn't face talking about it? Not then and not now? Had he chosen to ignore Grace's thoughts and feelings because he couldn't bring himself to talk about it?

He wrapped his daughter in his arms and held her like he never wanted to let go, reassuring her that nothing was further from the truth.

Autumn, sensing that they needed to be alone, said, "I'll go help Summer get all the kids settled down for a nap."

Before she could leave the kitchen, Grace turned to suddenly hug her. "Please save my family," she implored. "I know we just met you, but you seem very kind and understanding."

Spencer had the same initial impression of Autumn, but he was also still reeling after having discovered that she was the woman he had formed an odd, instant connection with from across a room filled with other attractive women. He felt like she had struck a spark that he thought had died along with Julia.

"I'll do whatever I can," Autumn said to both of them. "But you have to realize that it may not be enough."

Sam and Alex refused to go down for a nap, so Spencer took them home and made plans for Autumn to come over to their house later.

The minute they left, Summer started peppering her sister with questions. "Do you remember why you ended your engagement to Dallas?" Before Autumn could reply, Summer continued, "You said you wanted a fairy tale love story like Brody and I have."

"I never said fairy tale," Autumn protested.

"You know what I mean. How is a marriage of convenience going to help you find your Brody?"

"I have a confession to make. I met, well, not met Spencer exactly, but…" Autumn started to ramble and couldn't find the words to express her thoughts and feelings.

"How and where did you 'not exactly' meet Spencer?"

"Some friends of mine from work suggested I go to a speed dating event with them. Spencer was there, but the place lost power, and we didn't get to connect. But we had this—thing. It was like we locked eyes and…"

Now this was something Summer could understand.

"And everything and everyone else faded away?" Summer smiled, lost in her own memories of a backstage concert. Eyes meeting across a crowded room. Everyone else fading into the background. Feeling lovestruck instead of simply starstruck. Was it possible her twin had found her own meant to be in an unexpected place?

"Yes."

"That's all well and good, but why don't you just date the man for a while? I know Brody and I are the exception to the rule. Do you know anyone else who experienced love at first sight?"

"The man needs a wife. Sooner rather than later. And may I remind you that the only men I have dated recently only have one thing on their mind? An introduction to your husband. Maybe time will change that. And quite apart from that, did you see how sad Grace is? She seems more than willing to do her part, and Sam and Alex are too young to realize that Spencer and I just met for the first time today."

Summer knew when her sister made up her mind there was no talking her out of it.

"If I give Spencer three or four years, I will still have plenty of time to find someone who wants me for me, not someone just angling for an introduction to my famous brother-in-law. Someone who is convinced they are country music's next big thing."

"Who wants to be country music's next big thing?" Brody walked into the family room and sat down next to Summer. "I'm more than ready to pass down my cowboy hat, although it's true that Summer likes me to wear it when—"

"Please, spare me the details of your sex life."

Brody rolled his eyes and laughed. "Did she tell you the news?"

"I sort of blurted it out," Summer admitted. "I wanted to wait and tell everyone this weekend."

Autumn could tell from the look on her sister's face that she was both thrilled and exhausted. "Maybe there will be two announcements this weekend," she said, only half-joking.

"If you're serious about this, you can't keep Mom and Dad in the dark. When the truth comes out, they will never forgive you."

Autumn didn't want the subject to return to her offer to marry Spencer, so she instead asked about the new baby. "Any thoughts about what you're having this time?"

Brody said "boy" at the exact same moment Summer said "girl."

A discussion ensued about names, and they said they had decided that this time they wanted to have a gender-reveal party rather than be surprised.

When Leo and Lucia woke up from their nap, Summer announced that she needed one, and Autumn left to go home and think. She was somewhat impulsive by nature but also believed in making a list of pros and cons. And even though the cons outweighed the pros in this particular circumstance, that didn't change her mind.

The drive to Spencer's home later was fraught with anxiety and questions running through her mind that she wished she had taken the time to write down. She felt completely unorganized, which was totally unlike her.

His home was large and lovely, and she took note of the nice outside play area for the twins before she rang the doorbell.

Grace opened the door and rushed to hug her like she was a long-lost family member. "I'm so glad you're here!" she announced with great enthusiasm. "Dad is going to let me stay up an extra half hour so we can spend some time together."

Spencer felt relieved to see her, having spent the last several hours expecting a phone call saying she had changed her mind.

Autumn walked around the house like a buyer interested in purchasing it.

"How many bedrooms?"

"Five, although I use one for an office."

She counted in her head. Assuming the twins shared a room, Grace had a room and there was a master bedroom, which left one guest bedroom. They showed her around the rest of the first floor, and then Grace asked Autumn if she would like to see her room.

"Dad, you stay here and make Autumn something to drink." Grace sounded like the social director of the family.

Spencer smiled at his daughter's instructions and asked, "What would you like? Wine? Beer? Sweet tea?"

"Oh, I have an addiction to sweet tea." She licked her lips in anticipation, and Spencer suddenly wondered what they would taste like.

"We'll be back down in a few minutes," Grace said as she led Autumn upstairs to her bedroom.

"Dad let me decorate it myself," she said proudly.

Autumn had always been more of a tomboy, but she could tell from the décor that Grace was a girlie-girl. There were sheer white curtains blowing in the breeze against three butter-yellow walls. The fourth wall was a blank canvas.

"Haven't gotten around to finishing yet? I could help you with that."

Grace shook her head and turned her sad gray eyes towards Autumn. She pulled out a well-loved photo album and turned immediately to the page she wanted. She pointed to a photograph of a lovely mural. There was a garden scene with a gazebo, flowers in every color of the rainbow, and butterflies.

"That's beautiful. What am I looking at?"

"It was taken in my old bedroom." Grace's eyes filled with tears that threatened to overflow.

"Are you planning to re-create it here?"

Her voice grew soft and low as she shook her head and said in a voice so soft Autumn strained to hear her. "My Mommy painted it. I never wanted to leave that house, but Daddy said we needed to move."

Autumn leaned over to place both of her hands over Grace's rapidly beating heart. "You know that your Mommy will always live in your heart and your memories no matter where you live, right?"

"Daddy told me that, but Janet wanted to take her place. She told me I needed to grow up."

"Who's Janet?"

"Daddy dated her for a while before we moved here. One day he came home from work early, and she was packing up our family photographs."

Autumn had to think about how to phrase her response for something appropriate to say in front of a twelve-year-old. "She was wrong to do that."

Grace nodded, and what she said next both surprised and amused Autumn. "Daddy shoved her ass out the door so fast we thought she'd fall down!"

They had not heard Spencer's silent approach. "Grace, you know how I feel about language like that." Then he chuckled, and his smile lit up Autumn's world. "But in this case, you're right."

Chapter Four

T he twins were fast asleep, so Autumn, Spencer, and Grace went to sit in the family room. The fact that nothing looked out of place made Autumn a little nervous. She wasn't a slob, but neither was she a neat freak.

Spencer also looked nervous and finally said, "I have no idea how Grant and Laura made the leap from blaming me for Ben's tragic accident and Julia's death to thinking I am an unfit parent." It was obvious from his tone that he felt both hurt and confused. He looked around the room as though he expected to find the answers there.

"Which also begs the question," Autumn jumped in, "Why don't they want Grace too? How are they going to explain that to an attorney or a judge or a jury? I know your area of expertise is entertainment law, but I assume you have someone representing you in this. I find it hard to believe they think they could possibly win." Even though she barely knew him, she couldn't fathom what deep, dark secret he could be hiding that had led Julia's parents to sue for custody of Sam and Alex and not Grace.

She hesitated before asking this next question in front of his impressionable daughter. Even though Grace acted more mature than any twelve-year-old she knew, she was still a child.

"They don't have anything they are trying to blackmail you with, do they?"

Spencer shook his head. "Not unless they have some made-up evidence or a witness willing to lie. I have no idea what it could be. I did have relationships before Julia, but nothing serious. And once I fell in love with Julia, I never looked at another woman."

"Did you travel a lot for work? Did you miss any big moments? Grace's dance recitals or Ben's baseball games? Parent-teacher conferences?" Autumn could write a book about the damage absentee fathers could do to their school-age children.

"Our lives fell apart when Ben died. Julia, Grace, and I became our own little island. I know her parents were hurting too, and maybe they somehow blame me for the distance and how emotionally unavailable we all were those next six months. Julia stopped working. We had to force Grace to go to school. I moved to a smaller law firm that was more family-oriented and less concerned with billable hours. When the fog of grief lifted, we were all different. Losing a child rips a hole in your heart that never quite heals." He was distracted enough that he did not notice Autumn's haunted expression or the subtle shift in her body language.

"Don't you think a sudden engagement will seem a little. . . contrived?"

"My biggest client right now is your brother-in-law. My twins are close in age to Leo and Lucia, so it wouldn't be that much of a stretch to think you and I had met, spent some time together, and formed a connection that deepened once I came to live here. And if all that were true, anyone who knows me knows that after Janet, I would not introduce another woman to my children unless and until I was serious about her."

"So, are you thinking we'll get engaged, or that we'll get married quickly in a small, private ceremony? Which would seem more realistic, if all that were true?"

Grace, who had been silent up until now, offered her opinion. "I say get married. Don't wait."

Spencer replied, "I have never been the impetuous type, so I think a quickie marriage would raise more questions than a sudden engagement."

Autumn's mind suddenly and unexpectedly turned to thinking about a quickie, about Spencer thrusting into her with wild and uncontrolled passion. She had enjoyed an active and somewhat adventurous sex life but always wanted to be the one in control. She had never envisioned this scenario before.

It was difficult to get her mind back to the topic at hand. "Summer insists that our parents know this is not a real marriage, but I worry about too many people knowing, and the truth coming out. What about your family, parents, siblings?"

Spencer laughed and asked, "How long do you have?"

"Does that mean I need to take notes?"

"If you want to keep everyone straight, then yes. My parents divorced when I was younger than Grace, and both remarried and went on to have more children. My current stepfather, Curtis, has two daughters, and he and my mother, Barbara, have one child together, my half-brother, Matthew. My stepmother, Pamela, has one daughter, and she and my father, Charles, have one child together, my half-brother, Michael."

Autumn felt like she should be taking notes. "So, let me make sure I have this straight. You have three stepsisters and two half-brothers? Three girls, three boys?"

"Yes," he replied curtly. "But we were never the Brady Bunch."

"Once our marriage is over, do you see yourself marrying again? Starting another family?"

"Blended families work for some but not for others, and I wouldn't want to put Grace or Sam or Alex through that."

"Could you see yourself alone for the rest of your life?" Autumn thought that would be incredibly sad. She was somewhat younger than him but couldn't imagine why he would feel that way. Maybe he couldn't bear the thought of another woman replacing his beloved Julia in his heart and in his bed?

Spencer just shrugged. "I need to keep my head in the game and not think past getting over this hurdle. I need to make my performance believable, not just to Julia's parents but to my crazy family too. I don't care if your parents know the truth, but I can't trust mine with it." The problem was he knew it would be far too easy to make his performance believable.

So many different thoughts were circling through Autumn's mind that she was having a hard time concentrating.

"How many of your family members are close by, geographically? Is someone going to pop in sometime after the ceremony to discover we are sleeping in separate bedrooms?"

"My father and stepmother are the wild cards."

"What about your mother? How will she feel about you remarrying? Was she close to Julia? Does she spend much time with Grace or the twins?"

"My mother would like to pretend she is not old enough to be a grandmother. She's there for the big moments, but not the everyday stuff. She is close to her stepdaughters. She never hesitated to tell me when I was growing up that she was disappointed I wasn't a girl. So, she was probably disappointed when she had another boy."

"So, can I take that to mean you spent more time during your married life with Julia's parents and siblings?"

"Julia was an only child. I was already an adult when my half-brothers were born. It's not the polite thing to admit, or say out loud, but most of my adult life I still felt like an only child. I have little in common with either Michael or Matthew."

Even though Autumn didn't know that much about Spencer yet, she suspected they shared very few interests or similarities.

Grace interrupted and said, "Let's get back to the important stuff. Dad, you need to buy Autumn a ring and set a date."

Spencer turned to his twelve-year-old daughter, who at the moment sounded much more like a twenty-two-year-old. "Should we take the easy way out and tell everyone all at once? We could invite everyone here under the guise of hosting a housewarming party."

"Your whole family?" Autumn couldn't decide if she was relieved or upset that he wasn't close to his family, but in truth, it would make things easier. She would find it hard to lie to someone he was close to.

"And yours. You have three brothers, correct? Tell me about them."

"Adam is the oldest. He and his wife, Natalie, have two children. My middle brother, Carter, is dating a college friend of mine, and my youngest brother, Shawn, recently got married."

"Your family sounds much nicer than mine," he lamented.

That made Autumn laugh out loud. "Trust me, we have our moments. And when Brody fell in love with Summer, all our lives changed in an instant. But I didn't quite expect the impact that would have on my love life. Before Brody met Summer, he was concerned about someone loving him for him, not Brody the country music sensation, but I didn't think that would trickle down to me. The last three guys I dated were only interested in what I could do for them."

Even though she had said do "for" them and not "with" them, Spencer's mind went down that path anyway. He was stunned to discover that he wanted to explore Autumn's curves. There was something intriguing about her that he couldn't quite put his finger on, something he had felt the first moment he saw her. She was like an unexpected gift he wanted to unwrap.

Grace interrupted his thoughts and said, "Can we get back to what we are supposed to be talking about?"

"We have to lay the groundwork," he explained. "There are things we need to know about one another's lives and families if we want everyone to believe us. Before we plan an engagement party, we need to know more about each other. The big things. The little things. Is Autumn allergic to anything? Who was the first boy she kissed? Does she prefer dogs or cats? Things we would have talked about."

"How do you feel about telling your attorney the real story?"

"I want to play that out as it comes. I am hopeful that once Grant and Laura see us married, they will back off."

Autumn shook her head in disbelief. "I can't believe they think they stand a chance now. How old are they anyway? Late sixties? Early seventies? How old would Julia be?"

"Almost thirty-seven. And, as I recall, her parents had her somewhat late in life. So probably early seventies."

"And Sam and Alex are three? What judge in his or her right mind would think that was a preferable home environment, even if Grant and Laura are healthy now? That could change quickly."

Grace was so quiet Autumn sometimes forgot she was even there, so she was unprepared for her next statement.

"I'm surprised they don't want me. I could be their built-in babysitter." She said it with such sadness and bitterness that both Spencer and Autumn reached out to hug her at the same time, and Autumn rested her chin on Grace's head.

"That doesn't make any sense to me either. I know I don't know you very well yet, but for the life of me, I can't imagine why they would not want you too."

Spencer gave Autumn a grateful nod over the top of his daughter's head and mouthed a silent "thank you."

The three of them spent considerable time discussing when the party should be held and how much time they thought was realistic to learn each other's strengths and weaknesses, interests, and defining moments in their lives.

While they knew three weeks would be a stretch, that was what they finally decided on.

After Grace reluctantly went to bed, Spencer turned to face Autumn and said, "This is overwhelming. What if we slip up?"

"That will be the advantage of having my family be in the know. Any one of them would gladly step in and say or do something to get us back on track. Plus, let's look at it this way: you're an attorney, I'm a teacher. We both need to be detail-oriented in our daily lives."

They spent the next hour talking about everything under the sun: what it had been like for Autumn to grow up with a twin and have her twin marry a man who was a household name, Spencer's early career goal of wanting to be a sportscaster for ESPN, why he became an attorney, and what made her decide to be a teacher. It was a start.

They mutually agreed that Autumn's parents, siblings, and their spouses would know the real story. Autumn was relieved because she could not imagine having to keep that from everyone but Summer and Brody.

"I've always wondered what my parents thought when she announced out of the blue that she wanted to pursue a romantic relationship with Brody. I know they expressed their concerns about her dating someone so famous, but if they had more deep-seated concerns, they didn't express them to Summer."

"How did they feel about your former fiancé, Dallas? Were they upset when you broke up? Relieved? Disappointed?"

"Honestly, I think they were relieved when I broke off the engagement. I don't think they thought we were a good fit."

"Is that why you broke things off?"

Autumn sighed and decided she needed to be truthful. "I told them I wanted a man to look at me the way Brody looks at Summer. So, they would never believe the story we are going to tell everyone else."

It was almost midnight when Spencer walked her to the door. He thought about just taking her by surprise and kissing her. They needed to be comfortable with a small measure of romantic gestures, or they wouldn't be believable.

The same thoughts were running through Autumn's brain when she suddenly leaned in and kissed him. What was meant to be a brief experiment turned quickly into something more intense than either of them expected. He wrapped her in his arms and fully expected the fireworks to be going off outside instead of in his brain and his groin.

They mumbled goodnight. Autumn walked in a daze to her car, and Spencer leaned his forehead against the glass in the door to cool his thoughts. He tried to tell himself that his reaction was understandable since he had been celibate since long before his wife died, but that was not 100% true. He had never had such an immediate reaction to Janet, and when she started pressing him for intimacy, he told her he wasn't ready. Indeed, he had thought he might never be ready again. He wasn't sure if he should be happy or dismayed to discover he was wrong. How could he keep this marriage in name only when their first kiss ignited something in him long dormant?

Had he looked outside, he would have seen Autumn sitting in her car, too dazed and confused to drive away, reeling from their kiss in much the same way.

Chapter Five

Autumn wanted desperately to call her sister, but she knew it was far too late and she didn't want to worry her. She debated about sending her a text, but in the end, she just drove off, wondering the whole way home if this was how Summer felt when she first met Brody.

One of her college friends lived on the west coast, where it was only 9:00 PM, and she knew she could call Carly up until at least 11:00 PM California time, so she didn't hesitate. She could only hope she wasn't at work. She needed to talk to someone.

"What's up?" Carly answered with enthusiasm. "It's been far too long since we talked." They were both guilty of texting more than calling, partly because Carly was an ER nurse with a crazy schedule.

"I'm getting married." Autumn hadn't meant to just blurt it out like that.

There was dead silence on the other end of the phone and then a squeal of delight. "I didn't even know you were serious about someone! Well, after the last one. What was his name?"

"Greg."

"So, if it's not Greg, who is it? Someone from your past? Oh my gosh – did you get back together with Dallas?"

"Dallas is married, remember?"

"That's right. So, who are you marrying? It hasn't been that long since we last talked. How long have you been dating?"

"We're not."

"Not what?"

"Not dating." She took a deep breath and told her the whole story as she knew it.

"A marriage of convenience? In this day and age? Surely you're not serious."

"I thought it would be simple. Just a way to help a family stay together. And then…" she trailed off.

"And then what?" Carly prompted.

"I kissed him. It wasn't planned, it wasn't smart, but I wanted to get it over with. We'll have to be affectionate in front of anyone who doesn't know the real story. So, I thought I would test the waters, so to speak. And the next thing I knew, I was drowning in the deep end of the pool."

"So – you felt something when you kissed him?"

"I felt the earth move," Autumn whispered more to herself than to Carly. "It was like the last first kiss of the rest of my life."

"So, what you're saying is that you have feelings for this man."

"Yes, and it's terrible!"

"Why is it terrible? Maybe he felt the earth move too."

"I doubt it. He was married to the love of his life. He's looking for someone to hold his family together, not someone to replace Julia. And I don't want to be second best."

"A lot of people lose a spouse and go on to have a full and happy life with someone else. And how long are you supposed to put your life on hold for this man?"

"Three years, possibly four. But I don't look at it like putting my life on hold."

"You're always rescuing other people. Are you ever going to put yourself first?"

She'd had this same conversation with her siblings and her parents over the years. She'd rescued animals as a child, and in high school, she had always been the first one to befriend a transfer student. She went on mission trips in the summer and volunteered with Habitat for Humanity. She gave 100% to her causes, so there wasn't much time or energy left over to build a rewarding, satisfying personal life.

"I have to do this, Carly. Grace's sad face would haunt my dreams at night if I didn't."

"And what if you fall in love with him and he doesn't fall in love with you?"

"I guess I'll just have to live with it, however it turns out."

She knew if she told Carly she was already halfway in love with him, she wouldn't believe it. Autumn hardly believed it herself. Her twin had fallen totally head over heels in love with a man she married in a secret ceremony barely two weeks later. Autumn thought she was crazy. But Summer had known in an instant that Brody was her destiny. No man had ever made Autumn feel that way. Until Spencer.

Talk turned to Carly's work schedule and love life. She too had experienced ups and downs in the romance department, but always managed to remain positive. They lamented about the fact that they lived so many miles apart, and Autumn promised to keep her updated about Spencer.

By the time their conversation wrapped up an hour later, Autumn fell into bed but sleep did not come easy. Her dreams made her feel uncomfortable but oddly optimistic at the same time.

In the morning, she set out for the home of her parents, knowing she needed to be straight with them and wondering how they would take the news.

When she arrived, her parents were babysitting Leo and Lucia. Autumn watched them playing quietly for a moment as she debated about how to begin.

"What are you doing here, honey?" her father asked. "Not that we aren't always happy to see you."

Much like her sister before her, she just blurted it out without offering any background information first. "I met someone."

Scott and Leslie shared a knowing look. "This sounds a lot like the day your sister came to us and said she had met someone," her father said as though he wasn't all that surprised.

"Yes," Leslie agreed. "And then she announced he was someone famous. So, who is your special someone?"

"Spencer Sullivan, Brody's entertainment attorney." She knew they knew who Spencer was, but she started rambling, the words rushing out like a flood. "But it's not what you think. I mean, it's not like Summer and Brody."

"So, what is it like?" her father asked gently.

"He needs a wife."

"Why, in the 21st century, does he need a wife?" her mother asked.

She explained Ben's accident, Julia's cancer, her parents wanting custody of his three-year-old twins, but not his twelve-year-old daughter.

"Does he think they have any chance of winning? I would think trying to prove he was an unfit father would be an uphill battle with little chance of success. Have you considered that he might have secrets they have uncovered? Is it possible he is not the twins' biological father?"

Autumn's head was spinning, but if she was being honest with herself, the only thing that made sense was if Grant and Laura were suspicious he was not Alex and Sam's father.

Her mother continued where her father had left off. "Have you considered the fact that he might have painted life with Julia as being perfect when the reality was far different? Was she unfaithful? More importantly, was he?"

"I can't ask him that," Autumn did not hesitate to jump to Spencer's defense. "That's too private. Too personal."

"Don't you think you deserve to know the truth before you marry him?"

"This is going to be a marriage of convenience, not a love match. We aren't going to stay together; we aren't going to have children together. And while I grant you I don't know him all that well yet, I do know one thing. You can see the love and the pain in his eyes when he talks about her. I think I am a pretty good judge of character. There's no way that is an act."

After she left, there was one thing that Scott and Leslie could agree on: Autumn was quite quick to defend a man she claimed to be marrying only to keep his family together.

Three weeks later, Summer and Brody opened up their home for Spencer and Autumn to announce their engagement. Grace had offered to help her father pick out an engagement ring, but he said he had it covered, and before the guests arrived, he arranged a private moment alone with Autumn. His stomach was in knots and he felt exhilarated and oddly nervous at the same time.

"I know you were engaged before, and I hope once we go our separate ways, you will find the love you are looking for. So, this ring is yours to keep. Once we part, I want you to have it to remember us by, to remember the sacrifice you made for me and my children."

When he placed the ring on her finger, she felt like her heart stopped. She had not given him any hints about what she would prefer, other than it not being a diamond in a traditional setting. So, she could not believe he had picked out one she herself would have chosen. It was a beautiful sapphire, her birthstone, in a heart-shaped setting surrounded by tiny but brilliant diamonds.

"It's perfect. I love … it." While she meant it sincerely, those were not the three words she wanted to say. She kept the words of love locked in her heart, even though there were so many times over the course of the past three weeks that they had threatened to spill out. Every moment spent with Spencer, Grace, Alex, and Sam just continued to cement her feelings.

Most of her family were going to be in attendance, but Spencer did not know how many of his family members might or might not show up.

Spencer sighed and said, "I still think Summer and Brody didn't really think this through when they offered to host this gathering. Even though he doesn't tour as often he's still a hot commodity, and his female fans still go crazy at his shows, with careless disregard for the fact that he is a married man. I wouldn't put it past my step-sisters Lisa or Georgia to hit on him. Kelly is a lot more grounded. She's the only one I can really relate to."

"Not your half-brothers?" She found it interesting that he was closer to Kelly than the boys, even considering the age differences between him and his half-brothers.

"I've never spent much time with either Matthew or Michael, except for the occasional holiday. And I try to avoid those whenever possible."

Everything she was learning made her wonder that much more why Julia's parents were trying to take his youngest children away from him. Was there some big, deep, dark secret after all? Even though she had learned a lot about him in the past three weeks, she had barely scratched the surface of getting to know this man she was going to marry.

The weather turned out to be perfect for an outdoor barbecue. Autumn had reluctantly offered to help with the food, but her cooking skills left a lot to be desired. And since Summer spent more time in the bathroom than the kitchen, she hired a caterer.

Much to Spencer's surprise, more of his family members showed up than he had expected, although he knew some of them were there to get a glimpse of Brody. It had nothing to do with being there for him.

Autumn's brother, Carter, was there with his girlfriend, Angela, and her brother Shawn and his wife, Kyra. The only sibling of hers that was missing was Adam and his family.

For a group of people who were, for the most part, strangers, everyone appeared to be getting along fairly well.

Since Spencer had represented other musicians and somewhat famous actors over the years, his family didn't appear to be as star-struck as they might otherwise have been.

He wondered if Julia's parents had decided not to attend, which was just fine with him, when they showed up. Sam and Alex raced towards them with excitement, but Grace stayed rooted next to her father and Autumn.

Spencer was completely unaware that Autumn had reached out to Julia's parents prior to the party to try to smooth the waters if she could. Nothing could have shocked Spencer more than when Julia's mother congratulated him on finding love again.

"Grace is almost a teenager. She's at that age where she needs a mother figure," Laura said almost pleasantly. But before Spencer could say a word, she leaned in closer to whisper in his ear, "And of course, that will help her from missing her sisters too much when they come to live with us. Autumn is obviously young enough to give you more children."

As she walked away, Spencer found it almost impossible to rein in his anger and disbelief. Autumn had heard Laura congratulate him and was unaware of the turn the conversation had taken.

"Has Julia's father said anything to you yet? Laura seemed more gracious than I expected."

Spencer pulled Autumn aside, and she could sense the anger simmering beneath the surface. "It's all an act," he said through clenched teeth. "She thinks you and I can start a new family and replace Sam and Alex like they're nothing more than a pair of dolls."

Autumn's eyes came alive with anger and fire. He suddenly wondered what they would look like in the throes of passion and wanted nothing more than to find out.

"That bitch," Autumn whispered under her breath and took his hand. "Follow me."

Spencer didn't know what Autumn was planning, but he was willing to bet it would be designed to present a united front and put Laura in her place.

"I know this is a little premature," she turned to smile lovingly at Spencer, "but we've made our honeymoon plans and—"

Before Autumn could finish, Laura jumped in and said, "We would be happy to watch the children so you can have a nice, long honeymoon."

To someone who didn't understand Laura's endgame, it sounded like a nice gesture.

"What a lovely offer," Autumn answered with a smile when what she really wanted to do was take a swing. "But we have made our plans with them in mind. We asked Grace, Sam, and Alex where they would like to go, and we came to a unanimous decision. The five of us are going on a—"

"Disney cruise!" Sam, Alex, and Grace all screamed at once. The twins were jumping up and down, so excited you would think they were leaving that very day, and Grace hugged Autumn.

Before Laura could voice her opinion, Spencer jumped in. "Autumn was actually the one who suggested it." He smiled at his future wife with what looked suspiciously like both pride and love. "So, she deserves the credit."

"We need to start our married life out as a family." She knew the time had come to lay it on thick for Julia's parents, even though she meant every word.

"Grant, Laura, I want you both to know that I love your grandchildren. I want to be there for them, but I will never try to replace their mother. Our house will be filled with pictures of her and memories of her, and I want them to grow up hearing stories about her from you and their father."

Spencer found it difficult to control his emotions, both honored and touched by her words because he knew she meant every one of them. He squeezed her hand and said, "I feel very lucky to have found you."

Leslie and Scott watched from across the room and could sense the shift in the air.

"Something tells me this marriage is going to have a very different ending from the one they are expecting," Scott whispered into his wife's ear.

"And I hope he doesn't break her heart," Leslie added softly. "She never seemed as invested in the relationship with Dallas, and they had known each other for years before they got engaged."

"They were too much alike," Scott commented, not for the first time. "She needs someone to ground her."

Julia's parents left in a huff before the food was served and reminded Spencer that the following weekend they were expecting to have the children. He stuck to the once-monthly visitation schedule promised long ago to his dying wife, even though he was under no legal obligation to do so. Grace was getting more and more reluctant to go, and with the custody battle looming, he could hardly blame her. He didn't have any problem with allowing them to be a regular presence in the lives of their grandchildren, but the only way Sam and Alex would go live with them was over his dead body.

It was hard to turn his attention back to Autumn and their celebration. When she took his hand in hers, he knew she could sense his deep-seated concerns. He was confident he would win, but at what price to his children?

Chapter Six

The food was wonderful and plentiful, but Summer had a hard time keeping anything down. She and Brody were sitting with Autumn and Spencer, and the talk turned to her pregnancy. Summer was obviously both exhausted and excited, and Autumn was both happy for her sister and envious at the same time.

"Do you want to know what you're having?" Spencer asked.

"We do, but it's still too soon," Brody answered.

Spencer took a bite of one of the famous biscuits from the Loveless Café, and a look of pure pleasure filled his eyes and did strange things to Autumn's emotions.

"These are fabulous. Why have I never had them before? These are better than—" He struggled to find the right words when Autumn answered for him.

"Sex?" she asked, and everyone laughed.

"Then you have obviously been doing something wrong. These are good, but they aren't that good," Summer stated and gave her husband a naughty wink.

Spencer started to choke on his sweet tea as he wondered yet again why Autumn made him feel like his hormones were on steroids after just one kiss when he had never been the least bit tempted to take Janet to bed. He had no idea how he could keep Autumn in the friend zone for any length of time once they were living under the same roof.

When he turned to Autumn, he noticed that she had turned a shade of pink that made him wonder if she was thinking the same thing.

Before he could drag her off to a private corner and kiss her senseless, his stepsister Kelly joined them. As she was the only family member he felt close to, he felt guilty for keeping her in the dark. It was also true that she was the only one who knew Julia's parents had petitioned for custody of Sam and Alex, even though he knew most of his family members would be shocked if he told them.

Kelly smiled brightly at Autumn and asked, "Has this guy told you much about his crazy family?" She leaned closer to Autumn as though she was about to disclose a secret. "We're the only two normal ones in the whole group."

"I have heard quite a few… stories."

"Then you must feel a bit like you're joining the circus!"

"When my sister fell in love with Brody, all our lives took on a new direction. And ever since then—" she trailed off, not wanting it to look like she was somehow desperate to get married.

"Ever since? Don't leave me hanging," Kelly requested.

"The only men who have wanted to date me wanted just one thing."

Spencer knew what was coming, but what did it say about him that all he could think about was just one thing?

"Which was?"

"They all wanted an introduction to Brody. They all had dreams of becoming the next big thing in country music."

"Well, that's all behind you since you fell in love with my brother. Because, trust me, you do not want to hear him sing."

Spencer wanted to skip over the whole "since you fell in love with my brother" thing, so instead he said, "Have you ever heard me sing? Maybe Brody could use another backup singer."

Brody just smiled and offered to let him audition, which Spencer graciously turned down. "I wouldn't want to leave my new bride at home with the girls while I went on the road. So, thank you, but I think I'll keep my day job."

Spencer's mother, Barbara, and his stepfather joined them next. She hadn't spoken with them yet, and she could not help but feel guilty about all the subterfuge, even though Spencer was admittedly not nearly as close to them as she was to her parents. Autumn found it difficult to keep up the pretense. Fortunately, they didn't ask a lot of questions. She and Spencer still needed to come up with a "script." How had they met? When? They needed to cover more than just the basics.

By the time they finished talking to everyone, Autumn really did begin to feel like she had joined the circus. And she was more impressed than ever at how level-headed and normal Spencer was for having lived through a tumultuous childhood followed by undoubtedly difficult teenage years.

She felt a sense of relief when the party started to wind down and the only ones left were her side of the family.

When her brother Carter and his girlfriend Angela approached Autumn and Spencer, their hands were clasped tightly, and Carter, who was normally so self-confident, seemed at a loss for words.

"We didn't want to upstage you," he finally said. "So, we waited until everyone else left."

Angela couldn't hold back another moment. "We're engaged too!"

There were hugs and tears, much like when Summer had gotten engaged, and suddenly Autumn couldn't breathe. "I need a moment." She raced towards the house, and Brody had to stop Summer from going after her.

"Let her process," Brody said softly, and both Carter and Angela were visibly upset. They were the only family members that Autumn had not had a chance to explain the situation to, so her reaction took them by surprise.

"We should have waited," Angela admonished Carter. "But we weren't expecting that the news would be upsetting to her."

Spencer was also at a loss as to why Autumn had looked so bereft. Was she remembering her engagement to Dallas when it had been a love match?

Spencer gave her a few more minutes to compose herself and then went looking for her. He found her in the family room with the door half-closed, and he heard her talking to someone on her cell phone.

"What have I gotten myself into? You and I had great adventures planned. How can I tell him that I love—"

Spencer could not bear to hear her express her love for someone else. He would have to examine his reasons for that later, but right now he just knocked discreetly and walked in.

Autumn turned suddenly, and he couldn't help but think that she looked guilty. "I'll call you back when I get home," she said as she ended her call.

"A friend?" he asked innocently. "I hope you know you could have invited anyone you wanted to the engagement party."

Autumn avoided his gaze. "Did you need me for something?"

The sheen of unshed tears in her eyes was unmistakable, and the words rushed out of his mouth before he could stop them. "Do you want to back out? If you do, that's okay, I'll figure something else out. Maybe Kelly has a friend she could set me up with."

Autumn was momentarily confused but realized her reaction to Carter and Angela's engagement must have seemed odd.

"Are you not happy for them? Do you have some reason to think they shouldn't be getting married?" Spencer took her hands in his. "Or is this about us? If this plan suddenly seems too overwhelming and real, I understand."

"You've been married. You had a once-in-a-lifetime love. Julia was your wife, your best friend, the mother of your children. I thought I was going to have all that with Dallas, but we just didn't have 'it.' The elusive 'it.' We were compatible in most areas, and the sex was amazing." She was talking so fast she wasn't thinking about what she was saying. "But looking back, I realize we got engaged at the same time a lot of our friends were getting engaged."

"Do you regret ending the engagement?" He both did and did not want to hear the answer to that question, but it was too late to retract it now. Did her heart still belong to Dallas?

Autumn shook her head. "He's married now. Did I forget to mention that? The spring after we broke up, he went to his high school reunion and reconnected with his high school girlfriend, Gina. I heard recently that they are expecting their first child. The child I thought we would have. The child we were supposed to have until—"

It did funny things to his heart thinking about her having a child with another man. Before today, he had never permitted himself to think about making the marriage a real one, but now all he could think about was her carrying his child. But he knew if he expressed that hope out loud, she would run as fast as she could in the other direction. That was not their agreement, and he needed to remember that.

"Autumn, if you don't care about Dallas, I don't care about Dallas. But are there any other important relationships I should know about?"

She shook her head sadly. "No. I'm yours for as long as you need me."

"Then let's go back outside because I much prefer the company of your family to mine."

"Are we going to invite your entire family to the wedding?"

"Oh, no. No, no, no. I vote for a small, simple ceremony: me, you, the kids, a couple of witnesses. I know you would want your entire family there if this was a real marriage. This way, when the day comes that you do fall in love and get married, you can have the ceremony you deserve."

She mulled that over for a moment. It did make sense, even though it hurt her heart to hear him refer to their marriage as not being a real one.

"That does make sense. And if we don't invite my family, it won't seem like such a slap in the face to your family."

"Now we're on the same page."

The closer the time got to the ceremony; the more nervous Autumn became. They asked Summer and Brody to stand up for them. Grace, Sam, and Alex would be the only others in attendance. Autumn's parents weren't happy about being excluded, but they had assured her that they understood.

Spencer asked Autumn for decorating advice to make his house more of a home, but the truth was it was already pretty close to perfect. It looked like a family home, not a bachelor pad. There was a play area for the twins and a large eat-in kitchen with state-of-the-art appliances. Autumn didn't want to admit that she wasn't much of a cook.

Fortunately, the temporary nanny was a wonderful cook, but it had already been decided that Autumn would watch the children for the balance of their summer break once they returned home from their honeymoon.

One evening, Autumn went over to the house and attempted to make what she thought would be both an easy and nutritious meal but failed miserably. She got upset, but everyone else was amused, and that upset her even more. It didn't help matters any when the twins announced that they would much rather have pizza or chicken nuggets.

Spencer ordered a pizza, and when he went to pay for it, Grace took Autumn aside.

"Don't worry—our mom wasn't much of a cook either. We grew up with housekeepers who prepared most of our meals before they left for the day."

Something suddenly occurred to Autumn – a question she had never thought to ask before. "What did your mother do?"

"She was a hospice nurse."

How utterly tragic, Autumn thought, that someone who consoled family members or patients dying of cancer would be stricken with the disease herself. Her next thought was that someone should nominate Julia for sainthood. It was a good thing she did not have to try to compete with her memory or for Spencer's love. She knew she would fall short.

At the same time, Autumn worried about the chemistry that sizzled in the air whenever Spencer was near, but she had also learned from her relationship with Dallas that there was more to a stable, committed relationship than sexual compatibility. Looking back, she realized that she and Dallas had never really formed what she would consider to be a deep emotional connection.

When Summer had fallen in love with Brody, Autumn's reaction to her twin's happily ever after was not what she had expected. Yes, she had been happy for her. But she had also been envious. Not of his fame, or his wealth, or their lifestyle. She was envious that Summer had found the missing piece of her heart.

The week before the wedding, Spencer hired movers to get Autumn's things out of storage, in spite of the fact that she had told him they could just stay there. She hated to think about having to move her possessions back out of his house in a few years, but he was insistent.

"How would it look," he had asked, "if Grant and Laura come to pick the children up after the wedding and the house looks exactly the same? Don't you have some paintings or photos or souvenirs that you want to display?"

She agreed that there were a few things, but he got a strange look on his face when she talked about a favorite souvenir she purchased on a trip to Mexico with Dani.

The night before the wedding, Autumn found it hard to fall asleep. She tossed and turned, trying not to picture what it would be like to sleep next to Spencer, to fall asleep or wake up tangled in his naked arms. She did not want to be a replacement for Julia, but, she asked herself, did they have to forego intimacy if they were mutually attracted to one another? The only problem with that was she didn't know if he was attracted to her. He had not made any moves to kiss her since the first time she had kissed him.

Fifteen miles away, much of the same thoughts were keeping Spencer awake. That he desired Autumn was surprising but not unwelcome. He was too young to live life without the pleasures of sex. And they couldn't very well get an annulment at the end of their time together because then it would be glaringly obvious that they had never intended for it to be a real marriage.

Shortly after midnight, he gave serious thought to calling her to come over and spend the rest of the night with him. He didn't need to make love to her, although he wanted to. He just wanted to find out if she was having the same feelings and desires.

When Autumn's phone rang at 2:00 in the morning, she hoped against hope that it was Spencer, but it was a panic-stricken Brody instead.

"Mom came to stay with the kids. Summer is in the hospital. I'm worried she is having a miscarriage. You and Spencer will have to find someone else to stand up for you tomorrow. I'll let you know more when I know more."

"What hospital? Nash General?" All she heard Brody say was "yes" before he hung up.

Two minutes later, she was hastily dressed, on her way out the door, and calling Spencer.

When her number came up on his caller ID, he could hardly believe it. Was she thinking what he was thinking? Did she want him, need him, crave his touch the way he craved hers?

"I can't marry you tomorrow. Actually, I guess it's today."

His heart fell to the floor when she continued. "Summer is in the hospital. Brody is worried about a miscarriage. I'll call you when I know more."

She hung up before he could say a word. Even if he knew what hospital they were at, he couldn't leave Grace alone with the twins in the middle of the night.

Chapter Seven

Autumn arrived at the hospital to find her parents huddled close together in the waiting room, tears streaming unchecked down her mother's face. Her father's expression was grim.

"Is the baby …" she couldn't bring herself to say gone, but her mother nodded sadly.

"She's been asking for you," her father said, his voice choked with emotion. "I'll let the head nurse know you're here."

When Autumn went into her sister's room, Brody was trying to reassure his wife that there would be more babies, that her first pregnancy had gone smoothly, that the doctors had found no medical reason why they couldn't try again.

Autumn looked at her grieving sister and didn't know quite what to say. Even though they were as close as two sisters could be, it took her by surprise when Summer asked Brody to leave the room.

She took the seat next to Summer's bed and took her hand. Her mind had taken her to a closed off space in her heart, even though she knew it wasn't fair to compare her feelings of loss to those of her sister.

"I am so very, very sorry. I know thinking about the two children you have waiting for you at home should help, but I don't know that anything would help right now."

Summer tried unsuccessfully to choke back a sob. "I pray you never have to go through something like this. Losing a child leaves a gaping hole in your heart. Brody didn't want to know if the baby was a boy or a girl. Maybe he thought it would make the loss seems more … real. But I needed to know. It was a girl. I wanted to name her Eloise."

Autumn felt a vise grip her heart and her throat. She had kept her own secret for too long, and it was time to bring it out into the light. Maybe then she could move on to a place of understanding. Of acceptance.

"I suffered a miscarriage." She said it so softly that Summer asked her to repeat it. Summer shook her head in quiet disbelief. If someone had asked her yesterday if she and her twin had any big secrets from one another, she would have said no.

"When did this happen? Recently? Were you seeing someone before you agreed to marry Spencer?"

"No, it was before you met Brody. I had trouble very early on, so Dallas and I chose not to say anything. To anybody. I lost the baby shortly before the end of my first trimester. I named her Evie."

Summer's eyes shimmered with unshed tears as she tried to find the words to console her sister. "There can be other babies. Not, I know, with Spencer, but someday. You're still young enough to meet someone after Spencer and start a family."

Autumn shook her head, trying to find the strength to say the words out loud that no one except Dallas had ever heard. "There were complications. My chances of conceiving aren't quite zero, but they might as well be. So, you see, you and Brody need to have more children so I have lots more nieces and nephews to spoil."

Something suddenly occurred to Summer. "Is that the real reason you and Dallas broke up? Because you couldn't give him children?"

"No, it was just the final crack in the foundation. We talked around it for a while. I think neither of us wanted to leave while we were still mourning the loss of our daughter. But as time went on, it became apparent we weren't meant to be together. It might seem like an odd thing to say, but we were just too much alike. I think there is something to the old saying about how opposites attract."

"Like you and Spencer?"

Autumn chuckled and changed the subject. She didn't want to get any ideas. She didn't want to think, to hope, that just because there had been an initial spark before they formally met one another, it might turn into something more than a marriage of convenience.

"Mom is waiting her turn to come in. I'll go get her."

Summer grabbed her hand before she walked away. "I'm sorry we can't be there for the ceremony. You and Spencer need to find someone else to stand up for you."

"I know this is a sham of a wedding, but I am not getting married without you. We'll reschedule."

It was almost six o'clock in the morning when she left the hospital and drove straight to Spencer's house. It would take time for her to come to think of it as her house.

She was grateful she already had a key to the house, because she did not want to be alone.

A tired looking Spencer was in the kitchen making coffee, and he rushed to envelope her in a hug. They had only been this close once before, and she took comfort in the strength of his muscular arms. She could only imagine how good he would look and feel with nothing between them.

"How's your sister?" He leaned back to place a chaste kiss on her forehead when she suddenly brought his lips to hers in a searing kiss that left her trembling and him with an immediate erection.

Autumn reared back and apologized. "I don't know what came over me. I just ... need to feel alive."

"And I'm happy to be here for you." He desperately wanted to kiss her again but did not want to take advantage of her emotional turmoil. "So, fill me in. What's the news? Is Summer okay? The baby?"

Autumn lost control and sank, sobbing, into the nearest chair. She wasn't just crying for Summer and Brody. She was crying for Evie. The pain and loss had been locked away for years, and now the dam had broken.

"She's gone." Summer's daughter was gone. Her daughter was gone, and so was the engraved birthstone ring that Dallas had given her on Evie's due date. Even though she had guarded it carefully, when she moved her things out of their house, she couldn't find it anywhere. She never considered replacing it. That would have been too much like replacing Evie.

"I sent the minister a text when I got up. I told him we needed to reschedule. That's all we're doing, right? Rescheduling? Not canceling?"

"I want to wait until Summer is stronger. I know we could ask someone else, but I want to wait."

He breathed a sigh of relief, but before he could ask her about that kiss, Grace came running into the kitchen and stopped in her tracks when she realized Autumn was there.

"What are you doing here? Don't you know it's bad luck to see each other before the ceremony?" Even though Grace knew perfectly well this was not a typical ceremony, she acted as though it was. Partly to perpetuate the illusion, and partly because she so badly wanted it to be true.

"We have to reschedule, honey. Autumn's sister is in the hospital. She lost her baby."

"No!" Grace shouted loud enough to wake the twins. "It has to be today. We were supposed to stay at Grandma and Grandpa's house tonight. What will they say? What will they think?"

"You, Sam, and Alex can still go."

"I don't want to go. I don't want to go there ever again."

Autumn tried to calm her down. "I'll call them myself. I'll tell them there was a death in the family." Her voice overflowed with pain. "I know this is nothing like what you went through with Ben, but it's still a death, and that's the way people should treat it. It's not just a loss. It cuts deeper than that."

Spencer knew she was very close to Summer, but the depth of her emotion seemed more extreme than he expected, and he wondered if this was not Summer's first miscarriage.

"That is not a call you should have to make. I'll take care of it. I'll wait for a more decent time to explain. And you look exhausted. Why don't you go take a shower or a bubble bath or a nap. I'm sure you didn't get much sleep last night."

As much as Autumn needed some rest, she doubted she could fall asleep now that all the old memories had come bubbling up to the surface.

"Do I remember seeing a hot tub on the deck?"

"Yes, the previous owners installed it shortly before he got transferred. They hadn't even used it yet."

"Join me?" she asked innocently before her mind – and his – went in a different direction.

Spencer cleared his throat and tried to tamp down his reaction as he stumbled over his words. "Um, not this time. I'm sure Grace would be happy to keep you company to try to help keep your mind off everything."

"You should eat something first," Grace stated like she was the parent instead of a pre-teen. "Dad – make her your special scrambled eggs."

"What's special about your scrambled eggs?" Autumn asked as Sam and Alex scampered into the kitchen. "Do you put jellybeans in them?" The girls giggled." Or maybe chocolate chips? Peanut butter?"

"Mushrooms and spinach."

"Spinach, yuck," Sam answered.

Spencer got out the eggs and mushrooms. "In case you haven't figured it out yet, Sam won't eat anything that's green, and Alex loves everything that's green."

Grace ushered the twins out of the kitchen. "Come on, let's wash up before breakfast."

"She's had to grow up too fast," Spencer sighed. "Ever since Ben died, it seems like her childhood ended. We were all sad, lost, drifting. One day just sort of blended into the next. Julia and I tried to get her to talk to someone, to a child therapist, but she always refused to go. I didn't have the heart to force her. When we found out about the twins, everyone's outlook improved. Then her mother got sick, and our lives fell apart for the second time."

As difficult as this question was to ask, Autumn felt she needed to know the answer. "Would Julia still be alive if she hadn't gotten pregnant?"

"No one can answer that definitively. Her doctor doesn't know. I don't know. But her parents are convinced she would be. They never believed or understood how completely blindsided I was when she announced she was pregnant. It wasn't an accident, though. She obviously planned it. And I know she hoped to give me another son."

"But children aren't replaceable." The conviction in her voice surprised him yet again.

"You're right about that," he said sadly.

"And Grace is probably right. I should eat something."

As they were finishing their eggs, Kelly called to see if they needed anything, assuming the wedding was still on schedule. When she heard the news, she offered to come pick up the twins so Autumn could rest. Grace offered to go as well, thinking Autumn and her father could spend some time alone. Even though Kelly was not related by blood, she spent more time with them than anyone else in Spencer's family. Because of that, both Spencer and Autumn decided after the engagement party that Kelly needed to know the truth. Spencer needed someone besides Autumn that he could confide in, and he thought of Kelly like a sister.

By 9:00, the house was empty, and Autumn and Spencer suddenly felt uncomfortable being alone together in the house. They had spent time alone together before, but this seemed different somehow. They couldn't hide their mutual disappointment that the day wasn't turning out like they had expected. Autumn felt guilty about that, but so did Spencer, for an entirely different reason. While he had not expected they would consummate their marriage on their wedding night, he somehow felt it was inevitable that it would happen sooner or later. He was hoping for sooner.

"I think I will soak in the hot tub. You're welcome to join me if you change your mind."

Fortunately, the majority of her clothes were already there, including some swimsuits. She purchased a new one to take on the cruise, as her other ones were a little on the skimpy side, and she thought it inappropriate to parade around in a bikini on a family-oriented Disney cruise.

Before Spencer could place the call Julia's parents to update them, he saw Autumn walk toward the back deck. Seeing her in a lime green bikini, her hair piled on top of her head, made his heart race and his groin swell. The call could wait.

She was relaxing in the water with her eyes closed when she heard his approach. She opened them to find him carrying what looked like two glasses of orange juice in champagne flutes.

"Mimosas," he explained. "My original plan was to serve them tomorrow morning, but I decided not to wait."

Wait? Was now the time to tell him she did not want to wait—for anything? She felt like she had waited for someone like Spencer to come into her life for a long time. The future she envisioned, hoped for, was not the one they had planned.

Should she tell him she'd changed her mind? Wanted something more than a simple marriage of convenience? She couldn't find the words and it also didn't seem like the right time.

He handed her a mimosa and sat down across from her. When she took a sip and smiled with pleasure, his bathing trunks became uncomfortably tight.

"Delicious," she sighed. "You think of everything."

"Your lips look delicious," he said before he could stop himself.

"Then come over here and taste them." He wasn't sure if she meant it as a question or a command, but he didn't care. When he tasted her lips and swirled his tongue in her mouth, her body flooded with desire. He aroused a passion in her no man had before, but at the same time, she did not want him to want her only because she aroused a similar reaction in him. Even though some might call her outlook old-fashioned, for her, love and sex went hand in hand. She rarely experienced or enjoyed one without the other.

Spencer moved away, sensing that while her body might be willing, her heart needed time to catch up.

"I hope someone gives us an update soon. Any idea when they might release Summer?"

"Possibly today. I offered to watch Leo and Lucia, but the two grandmothers have it covered. They dote on them."

"That's what grandparents should do. When I was growing up, I spent every summer with my grandparents on my mother's side. Sadly, they've both been gone for a long time now."

"You must have had a somewhat lonely childhood. I can't imagine growing up without siblings to tease and torment and love and protect you. Do you think you might be closer to Michael and Matthew if not for the age difference?"

He sighed. "I was almost 18 when Michael was born and in college when Matthew came along." He often reflected on the fact that their family backgrounds could hardly be more different. "I don't imagine it was a picnic growing up with three older brothers."

Autumn giggled and said, "We used to make Shawn come to our tea parties. He's the closest to us in age. He even played with us and our dolls until Adam and Carter convinced him that wasn't something a boy should be doing."

She opened her eyes to discover Spencer's were closed, no doubt remembering his son and what he had been like as a boy.

"Do you want to talk about Ben, or is it still too difficult?"

"The people that tell you time heals all wounds have never lost a child. When I'm at the grocery store and I see a teenage boy, I wonder what Ben would look like now. Would he have been tall like me? Athletic? Musical? When he was five, he wanted to be a fireman."

"Don't most little boys?"

"What did five-year-old Autumn want to be?"

She couldn't tell if he needed to change the subject or genuinely wanted to know.

"I didn't have very lofty goals. I wanted to own my own flower shop. Summer wanted to write children's books. Now we like to tease her about being almost as famous as her husband."

He didn't sense any underlying envy in her tone or words. He knew her well enough to know she wanted everyone around her to be happy. Should he take a chance and tell her what would make him happy? He wanted to kiss her until she was as aroused as he was, and he did not want to stop until they were both satisfied and spent.

"Autumn …" He took a deep breath to try to calm his rapidly beating heart. "What would you say if I told you I wanted to—"

His cell phone took that moment to ring and break the spell. He wasn't sure if he wanted to curse, throw it across the deck, or thank the fates for intervening. If his feelings were completely one-sided, he did not want to give her any reason to change her mind about marrying him. He even thought about not answering it, but he saw Brody's name on the caller id.

"Brody, Autumn is right here with me. Talk to me. How's Summer? What do you need?" He listened for a moment and then nodded. "I'll be happy to call your agent. I have Evan's contact information. I can let him know you will be in touch about rescheduling some of your tour dates. You are absolutely right that the only place you need to be right now is with your family."

"Find out when they are discharging her," Autumn whispered.

"Brody, Autumn wants to talk to you." Spencer handed her the phone and got out of the hot tub to give her some privacy and clear his mind. Even if she was agreeable to what he had in mind, he could never take advantage of her while she was suffering.

Chapter Eight

B y the time Kelly returned with the kids, they were both dressed and making lunch. It seemed like a normal afternoon, one of hopefully many to come. He refused to consider the possibility that Grant and Laura could win. He just couldn't picture it coming out any other way than in his favor.

Kelly stayed for lunch and offered to stand up for them if Summer had a long, difficult recovery.

Autumn expressed her desire to wait for her sister. "I think for now we'll wait and see. The cruise is still three weeks away, so we don't need to try to reschedule that."

"Yes," Spencer pointed out, "because who knows what Grant and Laura would say if Autumn and I took the children on a trip and we weren't married yet."

"On the subject of the cruise—not that it's any of my business, but how many staterooms are you going to have?"

"One for Spencer and the twins and one for Grace and me. They're adjoining."

"Grace couldn't stop talking about it this morning. I swear she is every bit as excited about it as Sam and Alex are."

"It's nice you are so close to them," Autumn commented.

"That Grace is such a sweetheart. Did she ever tell either of you that at one point she thought I should marry Spencer since we are not related by blood?"

"No one would have believed that since everyone knows you are the sister I always wanted."

The devil on Kelly's shoulder made her ask, "But what about Lisa or Georgia?"

"I would rather have gone into hiding under an assumed name!" His expression turned serious as took both of Autumn's hands in his. "I haven't said this often enough. You're a lifesaver. I couldn't believe it when you walked into that kitchen and offered to marry me."

Kelly watched the glances exchanged between the two of them and saw something in their expressions she doubted either of them noticed.

"Tell me your backstory. The more you practice it, the more convincing it will sound."

Spencer began, "We met at Summer and Brody's house during my first trip here."

Autumn continued, "I was there visiting my sister and playing with Leo and Lucia when Spencer arrived with Sam and Alex." She smiled as though lost in a memory of something that really happened.

"I noticed how good she was with the twins, and I wondered if she was married with children of her own."

"And I noticed how attractive he was. And that he wasn't wearing a wedding ring."

"But we didn't formally meet, or spend any amount of time together, until I was in town again about a month later."

"And by then," Autumn added, "Brody had filled me in on his family history."

They went back and forth, telling their "story" and making it seem so real that Kelly would have believed every word if she didn't know the truth.

Two weeks later, Summer and Brody were ready to act as witnesses but suggested it would be easier on Summer if the ceremony took place at their house.

Their outdoor garden was beautiful, and it reminded Autumn of a smaller version of the gardens at the Grand Hotel where Summer and Brody had gotten married. She hoped that one day she might get to have her "real" wedding there.

The only others in attendance at the ceremony were Grace, Sam, and Alex. As soon as the minister pronounced them husband and wife and Spencer kissed her, Sam pulled on his leg and Alex on Autumn's. They looked up at them with identical sky-blue eyes and said in unison, "Can we call you Mom?"

Autumn looked panic-stricken, and Spencer looked heartbroken. Neither of them had thought to discuss this with the twins ahead of time.

Spencer knew if this was a real marriage, if he was planning to stay married to Autumn for the rest of his life, nothing would have pleased him more. But this felt more like an arrow straight through his heart.

Autumn could see he was struggling with what to say that would not hurt her feelings, so she took the initiative and bent down to their level. "How about for now you continue to call me Autumn, and once we spend more time together, we can talk about it again. Is that okay?"

The twins nodded their agreement as Grace looked on, unsure how she felt about this. It wasn't that she cared about the lie; it was more that she had already become close to

Autumn. Part of her was happy about that, and part of her felt like she was betraying her mother's memory.

Autumn saw the conflicting emotions brewing in Grace's eyes, and she reached out to pull her close. "I will always be here for you," she whispered in her ear. Even as Autumn spoke the words, she knew it would be a difficult promise to keep, even though she meant every word.

The morning before they were to leave on the Disney cruise, Grant and Laura came to pick the children up for the day. When they arrived at 8:00 a.m., Laura seemed particularly put out that Autumn was not there to greet them.

"Did you marry a party girl, Spencer?" Laura asked with a sneer.

Autumn stopped halfway down the hallway and decided to listen so she would know exactly what they were saying about her and what Spencer's response would be. But before he could say a word in her defense, Grace stuck up for her.

"She's been volunteering for—what's it called again, Dad?"

Steam rose from Spencer's nostrils, but he managed to answer somewhat civilly. "It's called Habitat for Humanity."

Grant looked impressed, but Laura scoffed at the notion. "A woman? Really?"

Autumn chose that moment to make her entrance. "Yes, really." She leaned up to plant a kiss on Spencer's cheek. "I stayed late last night because we were finishing up a house."

"What do you do when you're not volunteering?" Laura made it sound like a dirty word.

The whole dialogue disgusted Spencer. "She's a third-grade teacher, remember?"

"With training in infant CPR. I also have some EMT training," Autumn reminded her, wanting to add that if Laura ever got into trouble, she would be hard-pressed to lend her assistance.

"The children are ready to go. Please have them home by 4:00. Our flight leaves early tomorrow morning."

They returned promptly at 4:00. Grace got out of the car with the twins, and both Spencer and Autumn were relieved to have been spared another go-round with Laura.

The twins had never flown before and took in everything with a look of wonder. They were well-behaved on the plane and the ship, and everyone had a great time. Autumn and Spencer had even been able to take advantage of some adult only activities. Just not the ones that appealed the most to Spencer. But at the end of the seven days, they were all ready to go home.

On the plane ride back home, Autumn told the twins she had a surprise waiting for them and one for Grace as well. While the twins pestered her with a series of never-ending questions, Grace seemed both tired and moody.

A sullen expression clouded Grace's eyes and she couldn't suppress her thoughts and emotions for a single second longer. "I don't want to go home! That's not our home. I miss our old house and my friends and my school and my…." Her words trailed off as she choked back a sob.

"Mother?" Autumn asked quietly, and all Grace could do was nod her head.

Spencer was at a loss as to how to console his daughter when Autumn managed to come up with the perfect response.

"It's okay to miss her, Grace. You'll miss her for the rest of your life. She won't be there to teach you how to drive, dry your tears from your first broken heart, or see you graduate from high school and college."

"But neither will you!" Grace was crying harder now and starting to cause a scene.

Spencer didn't know what to think about her uncharacteristic show of emotion. She typically internalized everything, much like he did. While he knew it wasn't healthy for him, he did not know how to be more open or how to encourage her to be more open. He desperately hoped that Autumn, who wore her heart on her sleeve, would be around long enough to have a positive impact on all his children, but especially on Grace. They hadn't even been married a month, and he was already dreading the day when they would go their separate ways. She had brought the light back into their lives.

"Grace, honey," he said, "we'll be landing soon. Let's talk about this when we get home."

Grace dried her tears and nodded, but her heart still hurt. She remembered her mother, loved her mother, but had also made room in her heart for Autumn and did not want to lose her too.

When they arrived home, Grace asked if she could go unpack and take a shower. She felt uncomfortable and wanted to be left alone. She wanted to forget about her outburst. She wanted all of them to forget about it.

"What about your surprise?" Autumn asked gently.

"Could it wait until tomorrow?"

"It could, but since the surprise is in your bedroom, it will be impossible to miss it."

"Is it a puppy?" Sam cried out, clapping her hands in excitement.

"A puppy?" Not to be outdone, Alex asked in an even louder voice than her sister.

"No, it's not a puppy. No one is getting a puppy. But Grace, it's fine if you want to go to your room and call it a night." Grace turned away too fast to see the fleeting look of disappointment cross Autumn's face, but Spencer noticed it.

Autumn asked Sam and Alex if they wanted to go see their surprise, but before they could go upstairs to their room, Grace came barreling back into the living room and propelled herself at Autumn, almost knocking her over in the process.

"I can't believe it!" This time the tears she was crying were tears of joy. "I love it. I love you. It's perfect. Dad, Sam, Alex, you have to see it." She took her sisters by the hand, and Autumn and Spencer followed along.

Spencer was both curious and surprised. What could possibly have had this profound effect on his daughter?

He didn't know what to expect, but as he stopped in the entrance to her bedroom, he was floored. He could hardly believe the sight before him. There, in perfect detail and colors and brush strokes, was an exact replica of the mural from Grace's old bedroom.

"Who did this?" he asked with awe and gratitude and another emotion he hardly dared name.

"I made copies of the pictures from Grace's photo album. And then, I must confess, I managed to track down the family that bought your old house. Their granddaughter loved the mural, and they hadn't painted over it. There were even a few cans of old paint left, so it wasn't hard to match the colors."

"But who did this? I mean, I realize you came up with the idea, but who painted it?"

"The two art teachers in my school district. I thought about asking you; I should have asked you before I gave strangers access to your house—"

He stopped her with a kiss, the kind appropriate for their audience, but not the kind he wanted to give her.

"First of all, it's our house, not my house, and you don't need to ask my permission for anything."

"I did ask Summer and Brody to check on them. And, of course, all teachers have to be fingerprinted, so I figured it would be okay."

"It's more than okay." He kissed her again, once again having a hard time restraining himself. "You could not have done anything to please Grace more."

His show of emotion both touched and worried her. She knew it would be far too easy to convince herself that the playacting could become real. She was more than halfway in love with him already.

"Come on," she took Alex and Sam's hands and led them down the hall to their room. "Now it's time for your surprise."

She knew this would not have the same impact as recreating Grace's mural, but she was excited about her idea for their room also and hoped they would be too.

Spencer opened their bedroom door and was equally, if not more, impressed with what Autumn had come up with.

This she had done with no input from anyone. In that moment, he realized she knew his children almost as well as he did.

In their room, someone had painted scenes from their favorite book series, The Magical Unicorn, written by Summer.

"It's from the Magical Unicorn books!" Sam and Alex said with great enthusiasm and started jumping on their beds.

Spencer shook his head in disbelief. "I've heard you say that The Magical Unicorn books were inspired by Brody, but I have yet to hear why."

Autumn blushed and said she would tell him that story sometime.

"That's only the first part of the surprise," she told Alex and Sam as she reached on a high shelf in their closet to bring down two books. "This is the next book in the series called The Dancing Unicorn. It's not even available in stores yet. My sister gave me a very special advance copy for each of you."

The girls immediately quieted down and held the books reverently, their earlier exuberance gone in the blink of an eye.

"Will you read it to us at bedtime, Mommy Autumn?"

Tears immediately filled Autumn's eyes and Spencer's as well. Even though neither of them spoke aloud, they were each thinking the same thing. Was it fair to Sam and Alex to allow them to grow ever closer to Autumn when theirs was not a real marriage? And then there was Grace, who knew the truth but was attached to Autumn anyway. Even scarier than that, what if it turned into a real marriage for one of them but not both of them?

Autumn cleared her throat and bent down to hug them both." I'd love to."

"But first it's bath time," their father informed them.

"No, Daddy!"

"No?"

Sam and Alex each clutched one of Autumn's hands. "Mommy Autumn is going to give us our bath from now on. She sings silly songs to us."

They were insistent, and he could tell from the look on Autumn's face that she was pleased, so he gave up and went to his home office to catch up on some emails.

He got caught up in work and wasn't sure how much time had passed before he went to check on them. They were in bed, snuggled up to Autumn. He stood in the doorway until she finished reading, the twins so caught up in the story they didn't notice him standing there.

"Again, please," Alex asked, more politely than normal. They always asked for a second story and would pout if he told them no.

But Autumn just kissed the top of their heads and moved Alex into her own bed. "Not tonight, my sweet girls. Tomorrow we will read about the unicorn that went to the library."

Sam didn't put up a fuss and simply said, "I love the unicorns."

Alex, half asleep already, said, "I love you, Mommy Autumn."

"And I love both of you." She said goodnight and turned quickly before they could see the tears that flooded her eyes.

When she saw Spencer standing in the doorway, she brushed past him quickly. "I have something in my eye."

He let her pass, sensing she needed to be alone, and he went to check on Grace.

Grace was on her cell phone, talking to her old best friend, Kristy. "You should see it. You wouldn't believe it. It looks just like the one my mom painted. I'll text you a picture of it. How are Rachel and Jody?"

There were times when Grace seemed more serious since the move, and he knew she missed her old school and her old friends, but they had all needed a new start in a new town. He just hadn't expected to find a new woman there as well.

Chapter Nine

T he time was fast approaching to decide what they wanted to do to celebrate Ben's birthday. Grace brought the subject up with Autumn before Spencer could. She seemed hesitant to go with them, as though she did not feel like a real member of the family.

"I really don't need to be included," Autumn told him for the second or third time.

"And how would it look to Grant and Laura if my new bride stayed home?"

"I feel like Grant and Laura's opinions matter more than anything else!" She said it more harshly than she intended to.

"I just don't want to give them any ammunition."

"And I am starting to feel more and more like we were wrong to do this. Every day that passes your children get more attached to me, and I get more attached to them."

Spencer felt honestly perplexed. "Is that such a bad thing?"

"What are they going to do when I leave? They already lost their mother. I don't want to break their hearts all over again. You should have found a different way to fight Grant and Laura. What was it you told Kelly?"

"Go into hiding under assumed names? It's a little late for that now, and it's also a little late to re-think the wedding, even if it was a mistake."

He wanted to take the words back the minute he saw the hurt in her eyes. But he couldn't explain, couldn't tell her that his children weren't the only ones growing more attached to her every day. She had snuck into his heart when he wasn't looking. And it wasn't because of one big thing, but rather a million little everyday things.

She wanted to tell him how she was feeling, but didn't. Theirs was supposed to be a business arrangement, not a romantic entanglement. It wouldn't be fair to try to change the rules now, even though she asked herself every day how things might have turned out if he hadn't needed a wife. If he had gone to the speed dating event because he wanted to meet someone, felt ready to put his heart on the line again.

Instead of voicing her thoughts, Autumn returned to the subject of Grant and Laura. "Any word from their attorney?"

"I've got to think that he told them it is going to be more of an uphill battle now."

"Aren't you worried that they'll let it drop for now but start the action up again once we're divorced?"

"It's crossed my mind, but by then the twins will be in school, they will have friends and be involved in activities. And, hopefully, be old enough to make their wishes known."

Right now, the twins were like mirror images of each other. Autumn wondered what their personalities would be like once they went to school and made new friends.

"I wonder how their relationship will change and grow as they get older. Will they like the same things? Different things? I wonder if they will be more like me and Summer, or as different as night and day."

There never seemed to be any jealousy or resentment in her voice when she talked about Summer. He could only hope his girls would grow up to be as close, and he knew Autumn would be an excellent role model for them if he could just figure out how to get her to stay. He needed to find a way to weave her into the fabric of his everyday life. Their everyday life. He was not the only one who needed her. As he thought about how their lives could become more intertwined, he came up with an idea

"I know we had a small ceremony and no reception of any kind, so what would you think about an end-of-summer cookout? I'd like to meet your co-workers, especially the teachers that did the murals, and you need to meet some of the people from my firm."

"That's a great idea. Co-workers and friends, but not family, because Brody is the center of attention at any gathering simply by default. And what do you think about including some of Grace's friends? I heard her talking about a few girls she met at summer swim meets, Abby and Becca. Maybe include their parents? Have you met them?"

He shuddered involuntarily. "Becca's parents are great. Abby's parents are divorced, and her father recently got remarried. Her mother is a bit of a wild card."

"Flirt? Cougar?"

"Probably more flirt than cougar. And I know she's probably harmless, but she did make it known to me that she would be available for anything I might need or want. And I do mean anything."

"So, you turned down her proposition?"

"She seemed a little too desperate. And before you can ask, it never crossed my mind for a second to ask Tracey to marry me. She would have been all over me before the ink was dry on the marriage certificate."

"Probably before," Autumn commented, thinking he had no idea what a catch he was. Granted, he was the first widower she had dated, but based on her previous dating experience, she knew that men like him were few and far between.

"So, that's a no to inviting Tracey?" she asked with a secret sort of smile.

"Hell no, it's a yes. I want to show you off."

"I think you need glasses."

"And I think you need to start seeing yourself the way others see you. I love the light dusting of freckles on your nose and the flecks of gold in your eyes. When the sun shines on your hair, it looks like it's on fire. And when you smile…"

He came dangerously close to declaring his feelings for her, so rather than continuing to talk, he chose instead to demonstrate his feelings. He bent his head and kissed her thoroughly, tracing his tongue across her strawberry-infused lips. She tasted like heaven, and he wanted to taste all of her.

Autumn barely had time to catch her breath before he moved her close enough to feel his reaction.

She placed a hand on his racing heart. "Spencer, do you think this is a good idea?"

Rather than answer, he kissed her again. He finally drew a ragged breath and said with brutal honesty "I thought this part of my life was over. I didn't think I would find myself so overwhelmingly attracted to another woman after…"

She placed a finger on his mouth and whispered, "I know you loved Julia; you cherished her, raised children with her, buried a child with her, and expected to grow old with her. But knowing all that, knowing we will never have all that, we can have this."

"This? What do you mean by this?" He knew perfectly well what she meant but wanted to hear her say the words.

"This," she caressed the bulge in his slacks and leaned in to kiss him seductively. "The heat. The desire."

"The need," he whispered.

"The need," she echoed.

"I didn't plan on this. Didn't expect this."

"Neither did I. And someday we will have to get divorced, because if we file for an annulment, then Grant and Laura will know we never meant for this to be a real marriage. And who knows what trouble that might cause?"

He liked her reasoning. "So, what you're saying is that we should enjoy each other while we can. But I'm not ready for this."

"Oh, trust me, I can see that you're ready. And so am I." She felt like she had never been more ready in her entire life. The pool of desire that had settled below felt like it was burning her from the inside out.

"I meant I don't have any protection." If he had not been so aroused, he would have noticed her turn pale and struggle to respond.

"It's not a problem. I have that under control."

"Then there's nothing stopping us."

"Nothing," she agreed. "So, stop talking and make love to me."

"You need to know something first. It's been a long time for me, since long before, well, before." He did not want to mention his dead wife's name in the same breath as kissing Autumn.

"For me as well."

That surprised him. She was such a passionate, seductive creature. Someone who exuded sexual vibes so naturally that it was just like breathing. And the fact that she was totally unaware of her sensuality made her that much more desirable.

"And you should know I'm healthy," Autumn said, thankful for the yearly physical the school required.

He felt a little ashamed that had not crossed his mind at all. All he could think about was how fast he could get her out of her clothes.

"As am I."

She grabbed his hand and started down the hall to the master bedroom. "Then stop talking and do something about it!"

They practically raced each other to the bedroom, like two teenagers about to go all the way for the first time, and Spencer was worried that was exactly how he would perform.

When they reached the bedroom and he closed the door behind them, they shared a look of both passion and uncertainty. He wanted to make sure she didn't have any reservations about what they were about to do.

"You're sure?"

"Spencer, the moment you put your hands on me, I might go off like a firecracker."

She started unbuttoning his shirt so slowly he thought he might be the one to go off like a firecracker. As each button came undone, she pressed her lips to his golden chest.

"Your turn," he said, and just as slowly, he unbuttoned her blouse to discover a lacy, sexy bra, and his hands shook a little with excitement and anticipation.

"I've fantasized about this," he admitted as he bent to lick first one tight nipple and then the other. "Your curves are luscious."

It amused him to see her blush. "I'm glad one of us thinks so, because I could stand to lose a good fifteen or twenty pounds."

"You're just right."

As soon as she unzipped his slacks and began to caress him, he cautioned her about moving too fast.

"I want to make every moment count," he told her.

"And I want to get to know every inch of you."

They fell onto the bed, and she began to work her way down his body, stopping to kiss his chest and tease his belly button with her tongue until she claimed her prize. The minute she wrapped her mouth around him, he knew he was only seconds away from a mind-blowing orgasm.

"I want to—" he tried to talk but found it impossible.

She gave him a look like he was a naughty schoolboy and continued.

He struggled between closing his eyes in pure ecstasy and wanting to watch as his throbbing shaft moved in and out of her mouth in a game of fast-slow-fast. Unfortunately, it did end far too soon. He felt embarrassed by his inability to last, but she just smiled and kissed him with the taste of him on her lips.

"Now it's your turn," he said as he slipped a hand between her thighs to find her slick with desire.

"I've never been very comfortable with that."

"Then trust me when I say that was more spectacular than my fantasies."

"I meant someone doing it to me."

Once again, she took him by surprise. He would have thought she was more adventurous. But when he looked into her eyes, he guessed the answer.

"Do you like to be the one in control?" She nodded.

"Then how do you feel about me explaining in intimate detail what I want to do to you, and you can answer yes or no?" She nodded once again.

"Can I caress your breasts and cover them with feather-light kisses?"

It was hard for her to speak when every nerve ending in her body was akin to a raging fire.

"Yes."

"Can I get to know every inch of you from your belly button all the way down to…here?"

A trail of wet kisses down her body made her writhe beneath him, and all she could do was nod her head.

"Can I continue?"

Words failed her again, so she simply nodded.

His tongue found her heated core, and her world started spinning out of control.

"Spencer…" she pleaded, and he wasn't sure if she meant stop or don't stop.

"Tell me what you want."

She reached down to discover he was rock hard again. "You. Inside me. Now, Spencer."

When he thrust into her quivering body, she started to move in a way designed to send them both over the edge of the cliff. He tried to slow down, but the train was barreling down the tracks, and soon they both exploded in a single moment of colors and fireworks.

He lay down and pulled her close. His heart was beating like a racehorse that had just won the Derby. She pulled one of his hands to cover her heart that was beating as fast as his.

As they slowly relaxed and returned to earth, he wasn't quite sure what to say or do, wasn't sure if she wanted to spend that night and every night in his bed or return to her own room.

"Stay," he whispered softly against her ear, wanting nothing more out of life than this woman in his bed all night, every night.

Her only response was a soft purr of contentment.

They slept soundly, limbs intertwined, and were both more than ready to make love again around 6:00 in the morning. When they were done with round two, they were relieved neither one of them seemed to be experiencing any morning-after regrets. Spencer had been more than a little worried she would get up in the night to return to her own room.

They made their way to the kitchen to start breakfast just as Grace and the twins bounded in, still somewhat on overload from the cruise and their welcome home surprises from Autumn.

Sam and Alex were far too young to pick up on the charged atmosphere in the kitchen, but Grace picked up on it right away. Her father and Autumn seemed more in sync with one another. They shared easy smiles, and there was a hint of romance in their eyes when they looked at each other.

After breakfast, Grace helped clean up the kitchen, and Autumn announced she wanted to go visit her sister. The twins clamored to go along to play with Leo and Lucia, but Spencer knew Autumn was concerned about her sister's mental and physical health and needed to spend some time alone with her.

Chapter Ten

When Autumn arrived at Summer and Brody's house, she first encountered Brody, who seemed anxious, worried, and more stressed than ever before.

"I don't know what to do or say." He threaded his hands through his hair and shook his head with uncertainty. "I know she still needs time to grieve, but I also know this would have been far more devastating if this had happened with her first pregnancy. I tried to tell her I'd be fine if Leo and Lucia didn't have any brothers or sisters, but that just seemed to make things worse. I think what she needs more than anything is to talk to someone else who has been through this."

Autumn couldn't tell from his tone if Summer had shared with him that Autumn had also suffered a miscarriage in the past, but she didn't think so.

"I'll go see if I can lift her spirits. Where are Leo and Lucia?"

"My parents took them for the day so I could spend some time in the recording studio, but I didn't want to leave her alone."

"I can stay for a while. I'll let you know when I leave."

She found Summer curled up in the library in front of a roaring fire with the air conditioning on. Autumn had to laugh.

"Should I put on a sweater or take off my shoes?"

Summer looked at her crossly. "My next book is due in a week. I can't seem to get in the right frame of mind to finish it."

"What's it called?"

"The Magical Unicorn and The Fireman."

"Ah, now the fire makes more sense. This is what, book five? Don't you think your editor would give you an extension under the circumstances?"

"I don't want to have to tell everyone what happened," she responded sharply, then immediately regretted her outburst. "How did you manage to not tell anyone besides Dallas?"

"I could have handled telling you and Mom about the miscarriage, but not about the complications. I didn't want to hear that someday I might be able to have more children, advances in modern medicine, blah, blah, blah. The truth of the matter, which I did not want to fully face at the time, is that my chances of having a baby the old-fashioned way are very slim. I didn't want everyone feeling sorry for me."

"Does Spencer know?"

"There's no reason for Spencer to know. It's not like we have a traditional marriage and needed to discuss how we felt about having children of our own."

"Have you thought about what you would do if it turned into a real marriage? I see the sparks flying whenever the two of you are together. And now that I know about the two of you gazing at each other across all those other people at the speed dating event, it all makes perfect sense. Surely you must find Spencer attractive."

Summer had no idea how close to the truth that was, and as soon as Autumn averted her eyes, she gave herself away.

"You are attracted to him. I knew it! Are either of you going to do anything about it, or just go out of your way to avoid it?"

"Oh, we acted on it. The sparks practically set the bedroom on fire."

"Hmmm." Summer thought on that for a moment. "And here I pictured Spencer as the more the buttoned-up conservative type. So, who made the first move?"

"Do I ask you about your sex life?"

"No, but you could. There was this one time on our honeymoon. We were - "

Autumn covered her ears with her hands. "I beg of you, please stop. You two set off enough sparks to make me know you have an active sex life and trust me, that's all I need to know."

Tears suddenly filled Summer's eyes. "I'm not sure I ever want to have sex again. All I can think about is wanting to fill this house with babies and what if it doesn't happen?" Once again, she realized how selfish she sounded. "Autumn, I'm sorry. This can't be easy for you."

Autumn took a deep breath and said what she came here to say. "How would you feel about joining some sort of support group? I think I need to go too. I never really dealt with my emotions, my grief. Dallas tried to help, probably in the same way that Brody is trying to help. But for men, it's just different. They can't process the loss in quite the same way."

"Spencer would understand."

95

"And that's exactly why I will not bring it up with him. His loss was a thousand times worse."

"And worse than mine as well," Summer admitted. "If you find a support group, I'll go too. But how are we going to explain it to Mom and Dad and Brody? You know they will speculate about why you are going too."

Autumn put her head in her hands. "I can't think about that right now."

"Okay, we'll worry about that when the time comes. Let's talk about the Disney cruise. I'd love to go on one someday when Brody wouldn't be overwhelmed by fans."

That amused Autumn. "I think Leo and Lucia and however many other children you have, and I believe with my whole heart that there will be more children, will probably be old enough to give you grandchildren before that day ever comes."

Autumn at times wondered how high a cost Brody's fame exacted on her sister, but they never talked about it.

Autumn spent the next week completely moving into the master suite and watching Sam, Alex, and Grace while Spencer was at work. One night, a scheming Summer invited all the kids over for a sleepover so Spencer and Autumn could have the house to themselves.

When Spencer and Autumn got home from dropping the kids off, they were surprised to see Grant's car in the driveway.

"He's alone," Autumn observed. "As much as I dislike Laura, I hope something hasn't happened to her."

They both got out of the car and Grant approached them slowly.

"I was hoping to have a private moment with you, Spencer. Where are the children?"

"Spending the night with Autumn's sister, so now is as good a time as any. Let's go inside."

Autumn offered to leave them alone, but Spencer insisted that anything Grant needed to say he could say in front of her.

"Just spit it out."

"I've wondered for a while now why Laura is so hell-bent on wanting custody of just the twins. She claims … oh, Spencer, forgive me. She claims you aren't Alex and Sam's biological father."

Autumn thought back to her initial question about the possibility that Sam and Alex had a different father. But the more time she spent with Spencer, she found it impossible to believe. Everything she had learned about Julia and their marriage made her absolutely certain neither one of them would have ever cheated. Theirs was the kind of storybook romance you read about or saw portrayed in a movie.

"That's preposterous!" Spencer thundered. "Where is your wife?"

"She's having dinner with her sister. I thought I should come alone."

"Did she tell you why she thinks that? How can she possibly believe Julia had an affair?"

"She thinks you had one first, and Julia retaliated by having one."

Spencer could feel his blood pressure rising by the second and his cheeks flushed red with anger. "I am not going to dignify that with a response. The next time either of you hears from me, it will be through my lawyer. Grant, I have to ask you to leave now."

"What about our visitation schedule?"

"You and Laura are both well aware there is no legal, binding agreement. I did it for my children because their mother wanted it. But your wife has stepped over the line. I wanted to avoid a legal battle, but now I see that it is inevitable."

"So, you won't agree to a paternity test?"

"Hell, no. I want to see your wife perjure herself on the stand and present whatever so-called evidence she thinks she has. I'm sorry for your sake, but Laura started this. There will be no visits, no phone calls, no hanging around my house hoping to see them. If you force my hand, I can get a restraining order just like that!" He snapped his fingers to prove his point.

Grant looked truly upset with his wife and the situation she had created. "I begged her not to go down this road, but she's not listening to me. You've always been more than fair with us. I'm truly sorry."

Grant left, and Spencer stalked off to his office, the romantic mood ruined. Experience had taught Autumn that Spencer preferred to brood in silence, whereas she would call up a friend. She had put off calling some of her friends, finding it difficult to pretend her marriage was a typical one, but she owed a few of them a return call. She started with Lee.

"Hey, Mrs. Sullivan. What's up? How was the honeymoon?"

Autumn felt awful that none of her close friends knew the truth and she found it hard to try to sound like a normal new bride.

"Dani and I have a bet going that you're pregnant."

Okay, now she felt doubly worse, because none of them knew about Evie.

"No, sorry to disappoint you." She suddenly wanted to talk about anything else other than her life. "How's your new job as head of marketing?"

"Crazy. I don't know why I didn't turn down the offer. If Oliver hadn't wanted to stay home with the kids, I could never have taken on this insane schedule."

"How are the kids?"

"Jordan is about to start kindergarten, and Jessica is in the full-blown stages of the terrible twos. And yet my crazy husband thinks we should have another one. No thanks. I am so ready to be done with diapers, and I can finally sleep through the night."

What I wouldn't give, Autumn thought to herself, to have the opportunity to deal with dirty diapers and 2:00 a.m. feedings.

There was a loud noise in the background, and Lee groaned. "Jordan and Jessica started a band in the kitchen with the pots and pans. I better go in there before Jessica hits her brother on the head with one. Sorry I can't talk longer. Oh, hey, Oliver wants to say hello."

"Love you," she said, and then Oliver got on the phone.

"Oliver, text me your new address. Spencer and I are having a party before I head back to school, and I want to invite you."

Spencer hovered by the doorway, speechless to have heard her profess her love to someone and, in the next breath, issue a party invitation. He couldn't decide if he was mad or upset or both. Maybe all the mind-blowing sex didn't mean to her what it meant to him. On the other hand, undoubtedly Oliver lived more than a few miles away, hence the reason his name had not come up before. And he was right here, sharing a bed with Autumn.

Rather than letting on like he had been eavesdropping on her conversation, he went to the family room and sank down on the butterscotch-colored sofa. She followed a few minutes later.

"Sorry about earlier," he apologized and pulled her next to him. "I just needed to process."

"Me too." She moved her hand to his lap and was rewarded with his immediate reaction. "So, do you still need to let off a little steam?"

"That depends. What did you have in mind?"

"Do I have to spell it out for you?"

"I wish you would."

"Take me to bed," she whispered in his ear and told him exactly what she planned to do to him and with him.

He scooped her up like she weighed nothing and raced to the bedroom, where he proceeded to let her do everything she had suggested and more.

They were in the process of putting their clothes back on when the doorbell rang. Autumn hastily pulled her top on as Spencer went to answer the door. Neither one of them were surprised to see Laura standing there.

"In case your husband didn't pass along this message, you're not welcome here."

Autumn went to stand beside Spencer, and Laura pointed her finger at her. "You took up with this one awfully fast. Maybe she's the one you were sleeping with when my daughter was dying."

Autumn reached out and slapped her. She wasn't sure who was more surprised, Laura or Spencer.

"I have never laid a hand on a woman in my entire life, so fortunately I had Autumn here to give you what you deserve."

"Just one more thing I can use against you," Laura said smugly.

Spencer advanced close enough to Laura that she took a few steps back. "Do not attempt to ruin my wife's reputation with your outrageous fabrications. And for someone who proclaims to have loved her daughter, I cannot believe you think she was capable of betraying her marriage vows."

"You started it!" Laura shouted with a red face. "I know how estranged you and Julia became when Ben died."

"Get off my porch. Now. Or I'm calling the police."

"You wouldn't dare." Laura was sure he was bluffing.

"Oh, but I would." Autumn whipped out her cell phone, seconds away from dialing 911 when Laura backed down.

"You can't keep my grandchildren away from me forever."

"Maybe not forever, but for now I can. And in case your lawyer didn't see fit to tell you this, the courts are backed up. For months. Grace's birthday will come and go. And so will

Christmas. So, you go on home. But remember one thing. You started this fight. I didn't. But I will damn well finish it."

"This could all be solved with a paternity test, which I understand you refuse to take."

"I won't give you the satisfaction, and I won't move things along because you demand it. I did not want to drag this out, but now I do."

When Laura realized her aggressive behavior wasn't helping, she resorted to tears. "How can you be so cruel?"

Autumn had had enough, so she couldn't imagine how distraught and angry Spencer must be.

"The real question is how can you be such a heartless bitch?" Autumn spat out. "Calling 911 now. There is literally nothing I would enjoy more than seeing you in the back of a police car."

"I'm going. But you will be hearing from my lawyer."

"Bring it on!" Autumn and Spencer said in tandem, as though it had been rehearsed.

After Laura left, Autumn turned to Spencer and asked, "Are the courts really backed up, or were you trying to scare her?"

"They are a bit backed up, but I can tell my lawyer to drag his feet."

Autumn was both a little surprised and a little concerned. "Wouldn't you rather just get it over with?"

"That was my original intention. And much as my recent outburst might indicate otherwise, I don't want to come across as cold and unfeeling. But at this point, I also don't want to make things easier for Laura."

"I agree, but how long of a delay are you talking about? Weeks? Months? Years?"

"Doesn't matter."

"We wouldn't want to start divorce proceedings until the issue of custody was settled."

He was taken aback by her mention of the deal they had struck. He thought things were progressing in a manner that would make them both rethink the original deal. Apparently, his feelings for her were stronger than hers for him. Was it because the mysterious Oliver waited in the wings for her to be free? He had asked if there had been anyone serious since Dallas, and she had replied that there was not. So, who was Oliver?

Autumn could sense the change in his mood and wondered if he had started to see a future with her much like she envisioned one with him and the children. "Spencer – I just meant - "

"It's okay. It's probably best that we both remember the original agreement." His words were short and clipped, and she felt like crying. She wanted to stay and talk to him, lay her feelings bare, be open and honest, but it was not the right time. They needed to go pick up Sam, Alex, and Grace.

They spent the ride to Summer and Brody's house in uncomfortable silence. She wasn't sure what to say to make things right between them, and she didn't want to say the wrong thing and make things worse.

Grace didn't pick up on the tension because she was bursting with excitement. "Brody offered to give me guitar lessons. We're going to start next week. Summer said maybe

Autumn could bring me and visit with her." Her eyes pleaded with Autumn to agree. "Is that okay, Dad?"

"As long as it's okay with Autumn. Just keep in mind we'll have to make different arrangements once school starts."

"Count me in." Autumn agreed without a second thought. "I'd be happy to be your chauffeur."

On the way back home, the car was full of chatter, and Spencer and Autumn reached an unspoken truce. Neither one of them wanted to worry the children.

Chapter Eleven

When bedtime came, Spencer wondered if Autumn would join him in the master suite or decide to sleep in the room she had originally intended to occupy.

He had about given up on her joining him when she entered the room tentatively. She liked to wear slinky, sexy things to bed that he normally had off in less than sixty seconds, so he was disheartened to see her wearing an old college t-shirt of his that was several sizes too big and reached almost to her knees.

She stood in the doorway, uncertain as to her welcome. "I need to—"

"I want to—" he said at the same time. "Ladies first."

"I had a miscarriage," she blurted out.

Whatever he thought she was going to say, that was not it.

"What? When?" Was this what the Oliver connection was all about? He jumped off the bed to wrap her in a hug, wiping her tears away.

"Years ago. But until Summer lost her baby, I didn't tell anyone about it. Well, except for Dallas."

"Then Summer's miscarriage brought it all back up to the surface, didn't it?"

"Yes. And I agreed to go to a support group with her. It is way past time for me to try to heal. But I want you to know this—I know my loss is nothing compared to what you and Julia and Grace went through when Ben died."

"But it was your loss." He didn't know what to say to try to console her.

"It was a double loss."

"You were pregnant with twins?"

"No, I lost a daughter. But I also lost my ability to have more children."

"I'm so sorry. So, you don't think that maybe someday…" The words trailed off when she started shaking her head.

"There is no someday for me. And I'm afraid. I'm afraid that the more time I spend with you, the more I am going to want—" she choked back a sob and couldn't continue. She was right on the verge of telling him she loved him, wanted to stay married to him, wanted to help him raise Sam and Alex and Grace even if they could never have a child of their own.

"Going to want what?"

"A family of my own." She continued before he had a chance to respond. "I have a lot of thinking to do. As much as I would like to sleep next to you tonight, we both know I wouldn't have time to think or get much sleep."

He brushed a soft, sweet kiss against her forehead. "I hope being here with us hasn't caused you more pain. If you need to get back to your regular life for your mental and emotional well-being, I won't stand in your way. I don't want you to go, but you need to do what you need to do for yourself. You put us first, and now it's my turn to put you first."

And if that statement didn't just make her love him more.

After she left to sleep in the other room, he thought about what he could have said. What he should have said. But he didn't want a declaration of love to make her stay. It was true that he wanted her to stay because he loved her, but he also loved her enough to let her go.

Sleep did not come easy for either of them that night. Spencer knew he should be worrying about what would happen if Autumn decided to leave. He should be worrying about what a judge would think about a marriage that didn't last much more than a few months. But he also knew he wouldn't try to change her mind or try to stop her.

He decided to work from home that day. He wanted to be there to support her, whatever her decision was.

He started to make breakfast and thought about going to check on her when she walked into the kitchen.

"Mommy Autumn!" Sam greeted her with a hug, and Spencer cringed. He wasn't the only one who grew more attached to Autumn every day. Would his girls ever understand why he had made the choice he had? In his next breath, he had to ask himself if Julia would understand. Why he married Autumn, yes, but what would she think about how quickly he had come to care for her? How utterly impossible it had become to think about life without Autumn?

"Daddy's making toast!" Alex chimed in.

"French toast," he corrected her.

"Sounds yummy," Autumn rubbed her stomach and opened the refrigerator to get out the milk and juice. "What can I do?"

"Sit there and let me wait on you. I'm going to work from home today."

"Thank you," she whispered into his ear and kissed him.

As they sat in the kitchen talking and laughing and making plans for the day, Autumn knew she could never forgive herself if she left before Grant and Laura backed off, or their bid for custody got denied.

Grace was wise beyond her years and sensed that her parents needed some privacy to discuss whatever was on their minds. It shocked her to realize that that was how she thought of them now. They were no longer Autumn and Dad. They were Mom and Dad. She was both hopeful they would stay together and, at the same time, felt she disloyal to her mother's memory.

"Alex and Sam are the lucky ones," she whispered to herself, not meaning for anyone to overhear.

Autumn turned and asked, "Did you say something, Grace?"

Grace was too old to call her Mommy Autumn and wasn't quite ready yet to call her mom.

"I said Alex and Sam are the lucky ones. It's easier for them to accept … everything."

"Accept me?"

Grace nodded, a lump the size of a boulder in her throat.

"Grace, no matter what the future holds for your father and me, I can promise you one thing. I will not just up and disappear from your life."

"Never?" she asked hopefully.

"I can't promise never." Autumn moved to sit down next to Grace. "Someday, when I am no longer married to your father, he might meet someone in a more traditional manner and fall in love with her." Neither of them noticed Spencer hovering in the doorway, listening. "She's the one who will deserve to be called Mom. Having said that, Grace, nothing in life would make me happier than having a daughter just like you."

Tears filled Spencer's eyes, and he turned away. Her words touched a place deep inside his heart, and more of his resistance faded away. Every day, a little bit more of his heart belonged to Autumn, and soon it would be time to tell her that.

Before they knew it, the weekend arrived, and it was time to celebrate Ben's birthday.

Friday dawned a dreary, rainy August morning. They were fortunate enough to have rented a cabin for the weekend with two bedrooms, a loft, and a fireplace.

Grace was helping the twins pack, and Spencer filled Autumn in on what she could expect at the campground.

"We always try to get a place with a fireplace. Even if it's 90 degrees, we light the fireplace and roast s'mores. Ben loved s'mores. We've gone to the same place for the last few years."

"Sounds nice. Actually, it sounds perfect. I'm not much of one for roughing it. I spent enough nights sleeping in a tent to not care if I ever do it again."

"There's also a pool," Spencer added. "And yes, before you can ask, Sam and Alex started swimming lessons practically before they could walk. And, as you know, Grace is an excellent swimmer. She might even make the senior swim team this year."

"So, I should pack a swimsuit?" Autumn's eyes lit up with mischief.

"Please God, not the lime green bikini. If I close my eyes and picture you wearing that, I get an instant hard-on. Do you have a nice, sedate one-piece suit that covers everything up?" Even the less flashy one wore on the cruise turned him on. She looked good in everything. And nothing.

"So, no one else is allowed to ogle me either?"

He could tell she was just teasing him, but he didn't want to think about other men lusting after her. Julia had been a beautiful woman before disease ravaged her body, but she had never had the kind of body Autumn had been blessed with.

Autumn moved closer to whisper in his ear "Are you picturing it now? Untying the straps, taking my nipples in your mouth while I stroke you until you're ready to explode?"

He shut the bedroom door and locked it. "We'll need to be quick," he said as he began taking off her clothes. "And quiet."

When they were both naked, he picked her up, backed her against the door, and slid into her tight, wet folds. Their moves were frantic and unrestrained, and she clamped a hand over her mouth so she didn't scream his name when her release came on the heels of his, as it so often did.

"You still surprise me," she panted.

He grinned from ear to ear. "That impressive, am I?"

"That and more. But before it goes to your head, what I meant was that I am surprised there are fireworks. Every time."

"For me as well. You excite me. Delight me."

"At the risk of continuing to stroke your ego, let me say this: best sex of my life."

She started to pick her clothes up off the floor when he reached out to her to pull her in for a long, lingering kiss.

"Autumn, you brought me back to life." He cleared his throat. "This is about far more than just great sex, and we both know it."

He was on the verge of saying more when his cell phone rang. It seemed to her like it always rang at an inopportune moment and ruined the mood.

When he muted it, Autumn looked at him with eyes full of hope and a million questions. She knew she loved him in a way she had never loved anyone else. She wasn't his first love but wanted to be his last.

"It was Laura, again," he explained. "I instructed my attorney to file a restraining order. She just can't get it through her head that all communication needs to go through our attorneys. And yes, I know this will be a hard weekend for her. But she doesn't need to make it harder for me than it already is."

Autumn knew she needed to say something to lighten the mood. There were enough dark clouds hovering over all of them already, they didn't need more.

"I like making it hard," she said playfully.

Before he could reply, Grace knocked on the bedroom door and announced that she, Alex, and Sam were ready to go, and they all piled into Spencer's SUV.

When they arrived at the cabin, it was lovely and a bit secluded. When Autumn spotted the hot tub on the deck she raised her eyebrows, and Spencer got the message.

They took a vote and the children wanted to go swimming first.

When they got ready to go to the pool, Spencer pulled her in for a quick kiss. "You look hot."

"You have a wild imagination."

"Not really, just picturing the wild things we have already done, and the ones I am looking forward to doing in the not-so-distant future."

Sam and Alex splashed around in the kiddie pool, with a teenager keeping watch. Grace had her head stuck in a book, and Autumn and Spencer relaxed on beach chairs.

They hadn't been sitting down for more than five minutes when a man at least 15 years older than Autumn walked by very slowly and cast a long, lingering look of male admiration in her direction.

"Told you," Spencer muttered under his breath and kissed her hand. "Next, those college-aged boys will be getting out of the pool and strutting by you."

She found his unfounded jealousy endearing. "You're delusional."

"You have the body of a Playboy centerfold, and every man from 12 to 92 is going to notice you."

That made her laugh. "Be serious."

"I'll show you later just how irresistible you are after our cookout and s'mores."

"I think you need to cool off in the pool."

He stood up and led her to the edge of the pool. "Come with me."

"Don't I always?" she asked before shoving him in the deep end. Unfortunately, she didn't move back quickly enough because he grabbed her and pulled her in.

"Everyone is looking at us," she sputtered with a mouth full of water.

"No, everyone is looking at you and wishing they could trade places with me."

The afternoon went by quickly, and soon it was time for a cookout of hot dogs and roasted corn followed by s'mores. Alex and Sam were a sticky mess, and Autumn offered to give them a bath so Grace and her father could spend some time reminiscing.

Grace sat next to her father with her head on his shoulder. "I sometimes see a boy at school, and I wonder what Ben would look like now."

"I do the same thing, sweetie."

"He had your eyes."

"And his mother's smile."

"I'd like to think he and Mom are looking down on us right now. And I'd like to think she would like Autumn. You're happy for the first time in a long time. I hope you and Autumn stay married and give me a brother or a sister. Or one of each. I'm not picky."

Autumn walked in on the end of the conversation. "Grace," she tried to gently remind her, "that wasn't the plan."

"The plan. I know the plan! But I can also tell you two like each other because otherwise, why would you be having sex all the time?"

Spencer's eyes resembled those of a deer in the headlights, and Autumn was equally shocked.

Spencer found his voice first. "Are you sure you aren't 12 going on 30?" He tried to stall for time, hoping Autumn could come up with a suitable response to Grace's announcement. Apparently, they hadn't been as quiet or as discreet as he thought.

"Grace, this is really a private matter between your father and me."

"If we're never going to be a real family, then stop pretending like we are! Doesn't anyone care what I want?" Grace stomped out of the room.

"This reminds me of her outburst on the plane," Spencer said with a resigned sigh.

"Think we can chalk it up to her almost being a teenager?" Autumn asked hopefully.

"That may be part of it, but the other part of me knows we didn't really think things through. I never expected her emotions to get so involved, especially since she knows the real reason we got married."

Autumn desperately wanted to ask him how deeply his emotions were involved but refrained from doing so. This was an emotional enough weekend; she didn't need to add to his turmoil.

"Well, I don't know about you, but I'm trying to figure out how she knew we were having sex."

"It's those looks you give me."

"What about the looks you give me, like you're trying to figure out how soon you can get me naked again?"

"I think about getting you naked 24 hours a day. Even in my sleep."

Once again, Autumn asked herself if their relationship was more about physical pleasure than getting to know one another on a deeper level.

"Well, there won't be any of that tonight. It was an emotional day for all of us. I think we should pass on the hot tub and get a good night's sleep."

Autumn fell asleep almost as soon as her head hit the pillow, but Spencer's thoughts were full of his son, Julia, and what she would think about what he had done to keep his family together. He knew she would not have wanted him to spend the rest of his life alone, but he also hadn't expected Autumn to capture his heart. This marriage of convenience felt more real every passing day.

Chapter Twelve

He wasn't surprised when Autumn woke him up shortly before 6:00, having removed her pajama bottoms and sliding her hand inside his boxer shorts. Instead of their usual frantic pace, they made love slowly and reverently, and his heart fell the rest of the way.

Autumn fell back asleep, but Spencer got up to make coffee, his mind swirling in a hundred different directions.

The campground had kid-friendly activities throughout the day for Sam and Alex, and he was making note of what they might like to do when Autumn and Grace joined him in the kitchen area.

Neither Spencer nor Grace had gone kayaking before, but Autumn was an old pro.

"What other things do you know how to do?" Grace asked innocently and missed the look of desire that Spencer gave Autumn over the top of her head.

"My former fiancé, Dallas, and his brother owned a sporting goods store. Sometimes I got to try out new merchandise before they made a commitment to purchase it. Jet skis, snowboards, kayaks, snowmobiles, you name it, and I probably did it."

Grace looked at her with a bit of envy and disbelief. "Are you good at everything?"

Spencer's immediate reaction was to say yes, but he kept his mouth shut.

"Can't dance worth a damn. I have no sense of rhythm at all."

"I've never played an instrument before, but I am looking forward to taking guitar lessons."

After breakfast, they took Sam and Alex to the arts and crafts tent and went to see about kayaking. They got an instructor to go out with Grace, and Autumn and Spencer took out a two-person kayak.

"The kid looks barely old enough to drive," Spencer grumbled. "How much experience could he possibly have?"

"I asked. He's 23, and this is his third summer working here. Grace knows how to swim, and she's wearing a life jacket. You need to let her try new things. And, honestly, I'm more worried about you tipping over our kayak."

Fortunately, no one's kayak tipped over. When they were ready to return them, they overheard the instructor say to Grace, "Your mother must have had you when she was really young. She doesn't look much older than me."

"She's not." Grace wanted her father to notice the fact that other men found Autumn attractive. She was rewarded when she saw his eyes darken and pull Autumn in for a kiss. He was staking his claim, whether he realized it or not.

There was a bonfire that night, and each time Spencer got up to get more marshmallows or refill beverages, a different man would try to strike up a conversation with Autumn. He knew it was dark out, but couldn't they see she was wearing a wedding ring?

Spencer was returning when she waved the last guy off. "Married. Mother of three; just found out number four is on the way."

Spencer chuckled at her acting ability and congratulated her on it. "I'm guessing no one else will hit on you for the rest of the night."

"Not even you?" She kissed him to warn off anyone else. Their lips had barely parted when she said, "I may not be very good on the dance floor, but I have some moves in the bedroom that you haven't seen yet."

That was his cue to round up the kids and head back to the cabin.

The smell of the bonfire was clinging to everyone's hair and clothes, but Sam and Alex were half asleep and didn't want a bath. They did, however, want their big sister to sleep with them.

"We're going to stay up for a while," Spencer said as he tucked them all in.

"You can close the door," Grace said with a mischievous grin." We have our own bathroom, so we'll be fine. We're going to have a sister slumber party. No boys allowed."

Spencer couldn't help but think Grace was giving him permission to have sex with Autumn. He would have liked to explain to Grace that it went far deeper than that, but didn't want to get her hopes up. He was having a hard enough time trying to keep his own expectations realistic.

When they arrived back home, Spencer had three urgent emails from his attorney.

"Do most attorneys work weekends?" Autumn both wanted and didn't want the custody battle to be over for a variety of reasons. What would happen if Spencer suddenly didn't need her anymore? Would he ask her to stay, or thank her for helping him retain custody of his children and send her on her way?

"Luke is a friend. He wanted to give me a heads-up that tomorrow morning Laura is going to file for an emergency hearing."

"Is she lashing out because you won't let her see the kids?" Autumn had been afraid of what Laura would do if she felt pushed into a corner.

Spencer seemed to be taking it in stride. "We'll just have to see how it plays out."

When Spencer called Luke, he advised Spencer to accommodate her or she might get the sympathy of a judge. While he wasn't happy about it, he understood, but he was surprised when Autumn offered up an idea.

"I still have a few weeks left before I have to set up my classroom. What if you tell Laura and Grant they can come see the kids here at the house, but I'll be around?"

"I'll suggest supervised visitation and see what happens. I'm thinking she won't like it, but may have to accept it."

True to form, Laura did try to sway the judge in her favor, but Luke made a case for the supervised visitation, and the judge agreed.

Spencer was both thrilled and relieved about the outcome, and he rushed home to tell Autumn before he went to his afternoon meeting.

When he walked in, Summer was there visiting with Leo and Lucia. Autumn could tell from the look on his face that it had gone his way. But he still picked her up and twirled her around.

"I wish you could have seen the look on Laura's face when the judge told her they needed to come here to see the children."

"Let me know if you need me to come over and play referee," Summer offered. "Over the years I've learned how to deal with some of Brody's more aggressive fans, so trust me when I say I have plenty of experience putting obnoxious women in their place."

Spencer laughed, as did Autumn, but the look that passed between them did not go unnoticed by Summer. The emotions simmering beneath the surface were there for all the world to see.

The minute Spencer left to go to his meeting, Summer started grilling her sister.

"Something's different between you. Are you getting closer, starting to talk about staying together?"

Grace chose that moment to walk in. "They're in love with each other, but they are both too stubborn to admit it."

Words failed Autumn.

"It's okay, Autumn, I know you need to tell my father, but first you need to admit it to yourself."

The truth was she had admitted it to herself. Was it too soon to tell Spencer? She couldn't tell if he was struggling with the same question.

After Summer left with Leo and Lucia, Autumn enlisted Grace's help in the kitchen.

"I'm guessing you already figured out I'm not much of a cook. So, I need both your help and your advice. What is your father's favorite meal? Nothing complicated, please."

Grace thought about a few things her mother had taught her to cook as she got weaker.

"What about spaghetti?"

"Will you help me?"

Grace felt sorry for Autumn. For such a confident woman, there were things she had difficulty admitting she wasn't good at.

"I can, but let's wait until tomorrow. I can help you make a shopping list."

"Thank you," Autumn hugged her. "We can go shopping tomorrow, after I help Summer with something."

The support group meeting met with mixed reviews. Summer found it helpful, but Autumn found it utterly depressing. And they were both surprised to see a few men there.

After the meeting, they decided to go to their favorite café and see if Makayla was working. They both felt the need for pie and coffee.

Makayla congratulated Autumn on her marriage and said anything they wanted was on the house. They had known her for so long they considered her family.

"Connor seemed perfectly normal, but Tommy seemed like he was there to pick up women." Summer shuddered.

"I liked Morgan and Jenny. And if anyone realized who you're married to, they didn't act like it."

"I think it's kind of like AA in that regard. At least I hope it is."

"Summer, I'm not sure how many more meetings I can go to. Maybe once you feel more comfortable with the group I'll back off. Quite apart from the fact that I don't want to talk about my chances of conceiving being so dismal, I also don't have a normal marriage. Spencer and I aren't going to adopt; we aren't going to try in vitro."

Summer tried to be positive. "You never know what might happen."

"I don't need false hope. Besides, I don't know if Spencer would want more children even if it were a possibility. Grace is 12 going on 30, and Sam and Alex are almost 4. It could take years to adopt."

"Let's just take the meetings one week at a time," Summer suggested, hoping it would be beneficial to both of them.

When Autumn got home it was time to go shopping and make dinner. Autumn was saddened by Grace's capabilities in the kitchen. She had to grow up too soon.

Spencer was delighted to come home to the wonderful aromas coming from the kitchen.

"What are we having?" His mouth was watering.

"Baked spaghetti with garlic bread. Corn for Sam and broccoli for Alex." The twins had very different ideas about what vegetables they would and would not eat, and it had been a learning experience for Autumn.

When he tried to compliment Autumn, she gave all the credit to Grace.

"Mom helped," Grace said, the words out of her mouth before she knew it.

Spencer looked ecstatic, but Autumn looked nervous.

"That's very nice to hear, Grace, but maybe when your grandparents come over you should just call me Autumn. I haven't been married to your father for very long, and I don't want them to get the wrong impression."

"Oh, you mean that maybe you knew my father while my mother was still alive? Honestly, where does Grandma come up with this stuff?"

"I have no idea," Spencer said, trying to give Autumn a moment to compose herself.

It was one thing for Sam and Alex to call her Mommy Autumn; they were too young to remember their real mother. But hearing Grace say it almost broke her heart in two. She never thought she would get to hear someone call her mom.

Dinner was a hit, and so were the make-your-own sundaes they had for dessert. The kitchen was a disaster when finished, but it was worth the time and effort. Spencer was pleased there was enough whipped cream left for bedroom games after everyone else fell asleep.

The next day Grace was excited for her first guitar lesson. Autumn took Alex and Sam along to play with Leo and Lucia.

Before the lesson started, Grace turned to Brody with a serious expression. "Can I ask you something? Kind of personal?"

"I won't promise to answer, but I will if I can."

"Was Summer the first girl you loved?"

Whatever he had been expecting, it wasn't that, but he answered honestly.

"No, she wasn't. But she will be the last."

"Do you think there's a chance that Autumn and my father will stay together?"

He hated to dim the hope shining in her eyes. "I haven't been around them enough to be able to answer that. But it does need to be their decision."

"Did he ever tell you about Janet?"

"A little."

"I never really warmed up to her, but I love Autumn. I've seen the way my dad looks at her, and he never looked at Janet like that."

The lessons were fun, and Grace was a fast learner, so she started going twice a week. She also noticed how much Alex and Sam enjoyed playing with Leo and Lucia. Their families were so interconnected, and she didn't want it to end.

Chapter Thirteen

S oon it was time to plan the end of summer party, and while he wasn't happy about it, Spencer did nothing to discourage Autumn from inviting all her friends. Plus, his curiosity about 'Oliver' needed to be resolved, especially if he thought the other man might be potential competition for Autumn's heart.

The day before the party was the first scheduled visitation with Grant and Laura. Spencer offered to take the children to their house since Laura was recovering from a fall, and having difficulty getting around. While he didn't want to give them the upper hand, he also didn't want to come across as cold and unfeeling.

Autumn teased that he was just trying to help get out of getting the house ready for their party, but both her mother and Brody's mother offered to help. They had become fast friends, and Autumn wished she could find a way to bring Spencer and his mother closer together. She didn't want Spencer and the children to become their own little island once she was no longer in their lives.

Spencer arrived home optimistic that Laura seemed more reasonable, but Autumn likened it to a snake getting ready to strike.

Fortunately, the weather the following day dawned bright and sunny with only thin, wispy white clouds on the horizon. They both looked forward to mingling with each other's friends and co-workers.

The art teachers from Autumn's school arrived first, and Spencer thanked them profusely for the fantastic job they had done on the murals. He admitted to them somewhat sheepishly that he didn't have an artistic bone in his entire body.

More guests arrived, including some of Spencer's co-workers and their spouses, and his paralegal, Liz, who he credited with making his work life run smoothly.

When Grace's friends arrived, she took them in the house to see the mural. Seeing her excitement made Autumn's heart fill with gratitude that she had come up with the idea.

As the day progressed, Spencer wondered if the elusive Oliver was going to be a no-show when an unfamiliar man worthy of being on the cover of a magazine arrived. Spencer's heart dropped when he heard Autumn scream, "Oliver!" and take off at a run.

This was Oliver? Underwear model type Oliver with the kind of unruly hair women liked to run their fingers through?

In focusing on the man, he overlooked the equally attractive woman next to him, whom Autumn threw her arms around with abandon.

"I can't believe you're both here!" She dragged them over to Spencer's side.

"Spencer, this is my dear friend Oliver, and his wife, Lee."

Lee reached out to hug Spencer. "Yes, your wife and I have been friends for what seems like a lifetime, yet she never fails to introduce us as 'Oliver, and his wife, Lee.' For what, the last ten years?"

Oliver shook Spencer's hand and grinned. "That's probably because Autumn and I also go way back, and she introduced me to Lee. Lee originally thought Autumn and I were an item. Instead, she is the sister I always wanted."

Autumn laughed and compared her closeness to Oliver to that of Spencer and Kelly—family by choice, rather than blood.

Spencer felt like an idiot and did not want to admit to how many nights he'd spent tossing and turning, thinking that Oliver was a love interest from Autumn's not-so-distant past.

More guests arrived, and Autumn went out of her way to greet everyone.

Spencer tried hard not to draw comparisons between Julia and Autumn, but sometimes it was both unrealistic and inevitable. Julia had been more comfortable in smaller groups, but he compared Autumn to more of a social butterfly. He remembered the bonfire where the men had been drawn to her like moths to a flame. He couldn't imagine why she would want to spend her life with someone like him.

The only drama of the evening occurred when Lyle, the father of Grace's friend Abby, arrived with his new wife, Cindy, who was very friendly and down to earth. Autumn took an instant liking to them both.

It appeared obvious that Lyle's former wife, Tracey, whom Autumn had heard so much about, timed her arrival to coincide with that of Lyle and Cindy. Tracey made a beeline for Spencer, unaware that he was married. Autumn decided to have a little fun, even though Spencer's eyes were pleading with her to save him from Tracey.

Tracey clung to him much like her short, skimpy sundress was clinging to her when Autumn decided to save him.

"Honey," she purred, "I want you to come meet some more of the people I work with. Oh, hello. I'm Spencer's wife, Autumn. And you are?"

The looks Tracey shot Autumn were as cold as the ones she had given Cindy.

"I'm Tracey. A close friend of Spencer's." She made it sound as though they had had a fling at some point in the past, which Autumn knew to be wishful thinking on Tracey's part.

"Right, you're Abby's mother?"

"Yes, but as I was saying, Spencer and I go way back."

"That's nice, but he's mine now, so put your claws away." Autumn kissed him passionately to prove her point, then grabbed his arm and led him away, half expecting Tracey to follow along behind them.

Without an audience, Tracey didn't stay long, and Spencer complimented Autumn on her performance.

"Oh, that was no performance. No one but me is allowed to look at you like that."

"Like what?"

"Like they want to swallow you up."

That caused an instant reaction, just as Autumn knew it would.

"Save it for later when we're alone."

He wanted to round everyone up and tell them the party was over but refrained from doing so. He had never been as hungry for a woman as he was for Autumn.

When the night was over and the children were fast asleep, Autumn could hardly keep her eyes open.

"Hiring both a caterer and a clean-up crew was genius," she said with a yawn. "You have all kinds of brilliant ideas."

He would have liked to show her some of his brilliant ideas, but it she obviously needed sleep more than anything else.

Autumn closed her eyes briefly, and he picked her up in his arms to carry her to bed.

"I don't even have the energy to get undressed," she said sleepily. "But you could take my clothes off."

He wasn't sure if she meant that as an invitation.

"We both know where that will lead, and you're too tired."

Her eyes suddenly opened wide with fear. "Do you not want me?"

"I will never not want you," he promised her.

He turned off the light, planning to stay up for a while. He could tell from her breathing that she was almost asleep. He couldn't hold back the words in his heart even if she didn't hear them. They had been locked inside for too long. "I will go on wanting you for the rest of my life, even if we don't stay together that long."

He was almost out of the room when she whispered, "I love you."

He stopped in the doorway, unsure if she was even aware of what she had said. But he could not stop himself from whispering, "I love you too."

Autumn slept soundly, but Spencer tossed and turned, wondering what morning would bring. If she had been more asleep than awake, would she remember the words of love finally spoken out loud? Or, more importantly, would she choose to forget?

They were both still asleep when Grace knocked on the bedroom door. "Alex said she feels sick, and she's asking for both of you."

They got dressed in a hurry and found two pale little faces in their beds.

"My tummy hurts," Alex said, and her sister said the same thing.

Autumn felt Sam's forehead, and it didn't seem hot, but Alex was burning up.

Before Autumn could go in search of a thermometer, Grace held one out.

"You'd be a pretty good nurse," her father told her." Maybe you take after your mother."

The thermometer beeped, and Alex's temperature seemed extremely high to Autumn.

"Should we take her to the doctor? The emergency room?" Autumn panicked, wondering what she would have done if this had happened when Spencer wasn't home. Maybe she wasn't cut out for motherhood if a fever could send her into overdrive.

"We don't need to get too worked up just yet. I'm going to give her some medicine and see if the fever comes down. Then we can reevaluate."

Alex continued to improve throughout the day, and Autumn remarked that, fortunately, whatever bug she had, Sam had escaped getting.

"You may think that now," Spencer cautioned Autumn, "but usually if one of them gets sick, the other is not far behind."

"How do single parents do this? What did you do before you moved here? Housekeepers? Nannies?"

"Usually both. We had some great ones and some not-so-great ones. But, lucky for me, you came along and changed all that."

The real question of the day in Autumn's mind was what had she really changed? She was an okay housekeeper, a not-so-great cook, and when the children went back to school, Spencer would still need to find someone to watch them after school. She satisfied him physically; that much was obvious, but what about emotionally? She didn't expect to fill the space in his heart that would always belong to Julia, but was there enough room in his heart for her? So many questions demanded answers, but she wasn't ready to live with whatever the answers might be.

Sam did indeed get sick later in the day, and Autumn and Spencer took turns caring for her. It was the first time she felt like a real mother and hoped with all her heart that it would not be the last.

The twins went to bed earlier than usual, and Spencer wanted to do a little work, so that left Autumn and Grace to share what seemed to be an unnaturally awkward moment.

"Will you tell me more about your brothers?" Grace asked. "I wish I had been older when Ben died. I think it would be nice to brothers."

"I'm close to all my brothers, but Carter is the only one who lives close by."

"Do you spend a lot of time together?"

"When we can, but Adam and Shawn don't come home very often anymore, now that they're both married."

"Summer and your mom are great. I wish my dad's family wasn't so..." Grace struggled to find the right words and finally said, "broken. My mother didn't have any brothers or sisters, and neither did my father until Grandma Barbara and Grandpa Charles both got married again and started having new families."

"Is that what you're worried will happen with your father and me?" She hadn't really thought about Grace's feelings from that angle before. She was right that Spencer's family was, if not broken, at least fractured.

Grace nodded. "You've made us all happy, and I don't want to be sad again." She looked at Autumn like she could see right through to the heart of her. "Please give my dad more time. I know why he married you, but I think you've changed, and so has he."

Autumn went to a few more support group meetings with Summer, but she just wasn't getting much out of them. Everyone seemed to be a mix of hopeful and depressed. And since she didn't have any reason to be hopeful, that made her even more depressed.

Evie had not been planned. When they found out the news, she and Dallas were initially stunned, then excited, then devastated. The roller coaster of emotion took its toll on both of them. She knew if things had been different, he would have been a wonderful father to Evie, but they were not meant for one another. He found what had been missing when he reconnected with Gina. She had never expected to find it with Spencer.

Chapter Fourteen

Grant and Laura were scheduled to come for a visit, and Autumn stayed at the house as per the visitation agreement, but did not hover. Laura was getting around better, and Grace took her to her room to show her the mural.

When Laura saw it, she sank down on the bed, her eyes overflowing with tears. "Who did this for you?"

"Autumn did. Well, she didn't paint it herself, but she made all the arrangements. She even sent someone to our old house and found the right paint and everything. Grandma, why are you crying? I thought you'd be happy."

"I am happy, but it makes me miss your mother even more."

Grace's eyes filled with tears, and she felt closer to her grandmother in that moment than she had in a long time. "I miss her too, Grandma. I miss her so much my heart hurts. I know she was your daughter and you loved her, but I'm her daughter, so why don't you love me? Why don't you want me as much as you want Sam and Alex? Why don't you want me to come and live with you?"

"Oh, Grace dear, it's not that I don't want you, but I have reason to believe—"

"Stop right now." Autumn and Spencer had decided to listen in the hallway, both of them fulling expecting Laura to pull some stunt. "Grace, go with Autumn. I need to talk to your grandmother alone."

Autumn shut Grace's bedroom door and ushered her down the hall, shaken by what she had heard. It was one thing for Grace to wonder why her grandparents didn't want custody of her, but did that also mean she would want to live with them, given the choice? The subject had never come up. Did Grace want to stay with her father or did she just not want to leave him all alone since she knew Autumn planned to leave someday?

Grant, who had no idea what was happening upstairs, was sitting in the family room drinking coffee when Grace went rushing by him and went outside.

He turned to Autumn, who had been following Grace, and said, "What's wrong?"

"You need to put a muzzle on that wife of yours if you ever want to see those children again. She was about to tell Grace why you want custody of Sam and Alex, but not her."

When Grant made a move to go upstairs, Autumn stopped him. "Let Spencer handle it."

Autumn went into the kitchen to cool off when she overheard Spencer and Laura talking. She had forgotten there was a baby monitor in Grace's room as well as Alex and Sam's room. Before she moved in, Spencer explained that Grace started sleepwalking shortly after Ben died, and even though she appeared to have outgrown it, he wanted to be cautious.

"You cannot tell Grace why you want Sam and Alex and not her. The judge was very specific about you not trying to turn any of the children against me or against Autumn."

"Autumn," Laura spat her name out like it was a dirty word. "I don't know what you see in that woman. Well, except for the obvious."

Autumn waited for Spencer to defend her, but all he said was, "What is that supposed to mean?"

"You're a red-blooded man, and anyone with eyes can see she has the kind of body that fantasies are made of. You could have just had sex with her without marrying her."

Autumn couldn't believe Laura didn't suspect the reason behind their marriage.

"And what kind of example would that set for my children? Do you want them to see a parade of women coming and going from my bed and my life?"

"What happened to that Janet woman? Now there was someone who knew her place."

"Don't be so sure about that."

"Autumn thinks she has her hooks into my daughter's husband, but she will never fill Julia's place in your heart."

And there it was. Autumn's greatest fear verbalized. Spencer might want her, might need her, but she would never be Julia. She could live with being his second wife, but not with being the consolation prize.

She thought about getting up, leaving the house, and going for a drive, but her feet were rooted to the floor, her heart beating a mile a minute, her breathing shallow. She couldn't leave without hearing his reply.

When the words came, they were spoken so softly she almost didn't hear them.

"You're right about that. She will never take the place in my heart that will always belong to Julia."

Autumn choked back a sob. She grabbed her keys from the kitchen counter and raced out to her car like a serial killer was after her.

How could she have been so wrong, she asked herself. Was he just using her to get what he wanted—to keep all of Julia's precious children with him—and the sex was just an unexpected bonus?

Autumn knew in her heart that children were not replaceable, but she had to wonder about her other big fear. Might he feel differently about her if she could give him children? He would never forget Ben, and she would always grieve for Evie, but would having a child together change everything? If only it were possible.

She drove like the hounds of hell were after her, completely unaware that if she had stayed longer, she would have heard the rest of the conversation. Heard the words that would have quieted her fears.

"So, I was right," Laura said smugly. "You don't love Autumn."

"I do love Autumn," Spencer said vehemently, pointing his finger at her to try to make his point clearer. "I love her in a different way. She will never replace Julia in my heart. No one will ever be able to do that. But that does not mean that I can't love again."

"Do you plan to replace Ben too?"

"You might be hearing me, but you're not listening to me. I would never, as you put it, replace Ben."

Laura was unhappy that her plans to tell Grace had been squashed and left with Grant before even spending any time with Sam and Alex. She was always difficult when things didn't go her way.

Spencer went looking for Autumn, but Grace told him she had left. She hadn't noticed Autumn's frantic race from the house and had only seen her drive off.

Lunch came and went, and Spencer wondered why Autumn had rushed off without saying a word to Grace or leaving a note. But it never occurred to him that she had overheard any part of his conversation with Laura.

So, while he wasn't exactly worried, he became concerned because it was so out of character. He called Kelly and explained the situation, and she offered to come over so he could go look for Autumn.

When Kelly arrived, she asked, "Did you try calling her sister? Her mother?"

"Summer and Leslie are together, and she's not with them. I'm going to run by the school first. If she's not there, I'm not sure where to look next."

"I assume she's not answering her cell?"

"She left without it, which is also very unusual."

Kelly gave Spencer a look he had never seen on her face before. "Did you say something to hurt her feelings? Because if you did, you'll have to answer to her and to me. I admit I didn't have much time to get to know Julia well, but you should be thanking your lucky stars Autumn came into your life."

"I know!" he said with heartfelt conviction.

"If you know and I know and anyone else really close to you knows, then why doesn't she know?"

"Maybe because I'm terrified?"

"Of what?"

"Loving and losing another woman, another wife? I thought Julia and I were going to grow old together."

"Do not let fear stop you from giving your heart to Autumn. She needs to know your relationship is about more than just great sex."

Spencer put his head in his hands. "Does everyone know we're having sex?"

"When you two look at one another, it's written all over your faces. She looks like a woman well and truly satisfied, and you look like a man trying to figure out how soon you can get her back in bed."

Spencer, obviously uncomfortable, shook his head "We are not having this conversation. I'm going to find my wife."

"I know you can barely keep your hands off her, but try to tell her how you feel before you start taking her clothes off."

"Still not having this conversation," he said as he walked away.

As he drove along searching for Autumn's car, he replayed Kelly's comments in his head and thought about what he should say when he found her. Most men declared their feelings for their bride before the ceremony rather than after.

She wasn't at the school, so he thought perhaps she was indulging in some retail therapy. He drove around her favorite neighborhood shops and discovered her car sitting in front of a fancy coffee shop. He shouldn't have been surprised. She did love her frothy beverages.

As he approached the door, he saw her having what appeared to be an intense conversation with an unfamiliar man who reached out to place his hand on top of hers. She shook her head and pulled her hand away quickly, but she looked visibly upset. They didn't look like they were arguing, so he really wasn't sure what to make of the whole scenario. Was it possible that this man was Dallas? He'd never seen a photo of him.

He debated walking in, but it would seem too much like he was following her, didn't trust her. Plus, he was more of a black coffee kind of guy, and this was definitely not his kind of place.

He drove around for a while before he went back home. He told Kelly he hadn't found her, but she didn't believe him.

"You didn't find her, or you couldn't bring yourself to tell her how you feel?"

"You're too smart for your own good. I found her, okay? She was sitting in some fancy coffee shop with a good-looking guy."

"So, what does that mean? She's not allowed to have guy friends? You're my best friend and you're a guy."

"Hardly the same thing, and besides, I've met most of her friends. I've never seen him before."

"Maybe he's a new teacher at the school. Maybe he joined her because there were no empty tables."

"And maybe he joined her because my wife is smoking hot, and I'm not the only guy who pictures her naked."

Kelly appeared to be giving his thoughts some consideration. "She is that," she agreed. "Smoking hot, I mean. If I played for the other team…"

"Kelly, I'm serious. This guy was no stranger, and he was trying to hold her hands."

Kelly could tell Spencer was getting totally worked up. "I have an idea."

"What?" he practically bit her head off.

"Wait until she gets home and ask her who the guy was."

"Then she'll know I was out looking for her!"

"And wasn't that exactly what you were doing?"

"Yes, but I don't want her to know that."

"Men! Sometimes I don't know what to make of you."

"What does that mean?"

She picked her purse up and kissed him on the cheek. "It means I love you, but sometimes you are completely clueless."

Another hour passed before Autumn got home, and by then Spencer had worked himself into a frenzy. He didn't mean to pounce on her the minute she walked through the door, but he couldn't help himself.

"You didn't tell anyone you were leaving or when you'd be home." She looked annoyed, which just pissed him off even more. "Where were you? Out on a date you didn't want anyone – least of all me – to know about?"

"A date? Are you insane? I went for a drive. Then I stopped at my favorite coffee shop and ran into someone from my support group."

He had not expected her to lie to him, but neither could he call her on it without admitting he had seen her with Mr. Tall, Dark, and Handsome.

"How are those meetings going? You never really talk much about them, and I guess I just assumed you would if you wanted to."

"They're a waste of my time. Most, if not all, people are like Summer. They already have a healthy child, or they can still have a healthy child. I thought it might help, but honestly, it's just more painful. In case you haven't noticed, I have a hard time opening up."

"So, not even with the person you ran into at the coffee shop?" He hoped she would fess up to why she was sitting with the mystery man when there had been several empty tables in the coffee shop. It didn't matter if he was a friend, a new teacher at the school, or the brother of a friend. What upset him was her lying about it. If it was innocent, why hide it?

"No," she said crossly, and stalked off, ending the conversation.

Chapter Fifteen

When bedtime arrived, she offered to sleep in the other room. She complained of a nasty headache, which she tended to have more frequently when it was that time of the month. But he wondered if what she really wanted was for him to leave her alone.

"We can still cuddle," he said hopefully.

"You are the only man I have ever known who likes to cuddle. And not just to lead up to the main event. Which reminds me," she moved her hand lower to touch him and was instantly rewarded. "I love that my touch makes you so hard."

And just like that, he was. But two could play this game and tonight he needed to feel her, touch her, wanted her to feel the all-encompassing need. He knew there was no way she was sleeping with someone else. At most, perhaps coffee shop guy was a mild, harmless flirtation. He was also equally sure the guy had approached her, not the other way around.

"And I like," he said as he easily removed her impossibly tiny bottoms, "that I make you wet. You're the most passionate woman I have ever known."

It was hard to talk when his touch sent her into overdrive.

"It's almost that time of the month. Probably tomorrow —"

"Tomorrow I'll leave you alone. Tonight, I am all yours. Think of me as your sex slave. Tell me all your fantasies and I'll make them come true."

She burst into tears and when he moved to embrace her to ask what was wrong, she fled into the master bathroom and closed the door.

"Leave me alone!" she cried out in a wounded, pain-filled voice. "You can't make my fantasies come true."

He couldn't decide if he was hurt, shocked, confused, or all three. He opened the bathroom door to find her sitting on the edge of the tub and the words were out of his mouth before he could stop them.

"But someone else can?"

She blinked back the tears and looked at him, eyes wide with shock. "There's no one else. What are you talking about?"

"If there's no one else, then who was the man in the coffee shop?"

If she hadn't been so distraught, she would have asked how he knew it was a man she ran into at the coffee shop. He continued before she could respond.

"Autumn, I don't care who the man in the coffee shop was, but I do care that you chose to lie to me about it."

She pushed past him and went back into the bedroom. "If you can stand there and accuse me of lying, then you don't know me at all."

He thought about backing off, but for his own peace of mind, he needed answers. Truthful answers. He was here under the same roof with her, night, and day. He wasn't worried about some competition, but he was worried about why she chose to be secretive about it.

"I want a name, Autumn," he said in a voice he hardly recognized as his own.

"Connor. Connor Jackson, okay? And he is in my support group. There are only two men in the group. Tommy, the other guy, is a train wreck. His wife just left him after her third miscarriage. Personally, I think he joined the group hoping to find some woman desperate enough to sleep with him. Connor's wife just suffered her second miscarriage. He wants to keep trying. She doesn't. He joined the group to try to better understand the female perspective."

Spencer was deeply ashamed he had accused her of lying to him.

"Autumn, I'm so sorry. I know it doesn't excuse what I said. All I can say in my defense is that I was crazy with jealousy."

She shook with fury and lashed back. "How could you think I was capable of going behind your back and going out with someone else?" She picked up her phone and pulled up some photos. "Look, this is the guy you saw me with, right?" Without waiting for confirmation, she continued. "See, here's Connor's Facebook page. There's Connor with his wife, Amy."

"Then why did you burst into tears and tell me I couldn't make your fantasies come true?" None of this was making sense to Spencer.

"Because my fantasy is to have a baby, okay? Not just a baby – your baby. I want to get pregnant the old-fashioned way. I want to be able to track my ovulation, my fertile days. I want you to come to my doctor appointments with me and hold my hand when we hear the baby's heartbeat for the first time. Decide if we do or don't want to know the sex of the baby. Drive to the store at midnight because I want the only kind of ice cream we don't have in the freezer."

He suddenly realized that she had reacted the way she had because she was in love with him.

"You love me," he said in a voice full of wonder and reverence.

"I do love you," she said but quickly moved away when he reached out to embrace her. "But I can't be with a man who doesn't trust me. And on top of everything else, I heard what you said to Laura today, so now it's your turn to tell me the truth. And don't lie to me, Spencer, because I heard what you said. I heard you tell Laura that I could never fill the place in your heart that will always belong to Julia."

"I loved Julia. She was the first woman I ever truly loved. And you and I both know that you wouldn't be here if she hadn't died. It's hard for me to walk the line between trying to respect her memory while making new memories with you."

"I don't expect to take her place. In your life or in the lives of your children. I just need to know there is room in your heart for both of us."

"And you need to know that I love you every bit as much as I loved Julia. I love you in a different way that is no less real. When Julia and I first got married, we were both concentrating on our careers. She had a crazier schedule than I did, and there was no chance for being spontaneous. We had Ben and then Grace, and after we lost Ben ... life just wasn't the same anymore. You are the first woman I ever lusted after, ever went crazy over when another man looked at you like he was wondering what you'd be like in bed."

"What are you trying to say? That our relationship is more about passion than a lasting lifetime kind of love?"

"No. What I'm trying to say is that we can have both. And I've never had both before."

"I want to believe that, but I'm not sure I can."

"Then tell me what I can do to convince you," he pleaded with hands folded together in a silent prayer.

"You need to woo me, Spencer. You need to court me. You need to do all the things you would have done if we had met in a traditional way. Or an untraditional way, like the speed dating event. I want you to take me on dates and send me flowers. Write me love notes. And then after we know each other on a deeper level, I will think about returning to your bed."

"So, separate bedrooms?" God, he was going to go crazy without being able to touch her, taste her, feel her lips wrapped around him. He had been celibate for a long time, but the first time he had made love to Autumn, she ignited a fire that he knew would never go out. "You're sure there's nothing I can do to convince you of one more night of passion before we take a step back?"

"No," she said, like a prim spinster. "I mean yes. Yes to separate bedrooms."

"And as to my other question?"

"Spencer, I know what you're trying to do, and it won't work."

"Are you sure?"

From the look of indecisiveness on her face, he thought she'd give in, but she simply shook her head and said, "Yes."

He gave her a chaste kiss and said good night. She couldn't decide if she was happy or disappointed that he didn't try harder to change her mind.

Autumn had started getting up a little earlier each morning to get more used to her school routine, so Spencer was aware of what time her alarm normally went off. She was about to get out of bed when there was a knock on her door.

"Room service," he said in a British sounding accent.

"Come in."

He walked in with a breakfast tray holding a single red rose, a glass of orange juice, and an English muffin spread with her favorite strawberry preserves from the Loveless Café. Somehow, she had expected breakfast for two.

"Aren't you hungry?"

He leaned over to kiss her and brush a finger against one sensitive nipple. "Just for you, my love. Enjoy your breakfast while I go take a very cold shower."

It was Autumn's last day of total freedom before the new school year started, and she was debating what to do when Summer called her.

"Raven is in town and wants to see us. We're all going to the zoo. Do you want to come? You can bring Spencer and the kids, of course. Brody arranged for them to close down for two hours so he won't be mobbed with fans. You in?"

"Sure—let me check with Spencer and get back to you shortly."

When Spencer's cell phone rang, he didn't expect it to be Autumn.

"Autumn! How nice to hear your voice. Did you have breakfast already, or would you like to come over and eat my —"

"Spencer! We don't know each other well enough for that yet." He chuckled, and she continued. "Can you play hooky today and go to the zoo with my family?"

"I can rearrange my schedule. Can I pick you up?" By now, they were both laughing. "It's not like we can all fit in your car."

"Hey—don't make fun of Scarlett."

"Scarlett? Seriously? You name your vehicles?" This was something he had never heard her mention before, and he suddenly realized there were hundreds of little things he didn't know about her and she didn't know about him.

"Don't make fun of me. Everyone in my family does it."

"Okay. Well, getting back to the subject at hand, do you want to meet here? What time?"

"Let's say 10:00."

"I'll be waiting for you to come. I mean show up." It was amazing how many of their conversations had sexual undertones.

When 9:45 arrived, Autumn rang the doorbell. When Grace opened the door, she was confused and turned to her father.

"What's going on?"

"Autumn and I have decided it's high time we got to know each other on a different level."

Grace wasn't sure what he meant, and she raised her eyebrows questioningly.

"So, what does that mean, exactly?"

"We're going back to the beginning," Autumn explained. "We skipped the dating stage and went directly to married life. So now we are going to go on dates. Movies. Dinner."

"Dancing," Spencer couldn't resist adding.

"I'll consider it if you go to the ballet with me."

"Men in tights?" he shuddered.

"Relationships take compromise. You know—give and take."

His mind immediately went to her taking him for a ride and giving him all of herself, her body, her attention, while he gave her pleasure. And he could tell from her pink cheeks that she was thinking the exact same thing.

"Okay, kids. Let's go pile into the SUV. We're meeting everyone at the zoo."

Chapter Sixteen

On the way to the zoo, Spencer and Autumn sat in the front seat holding hands.

"Remind me again who Raven is," Spencer said. "This is one of those times when I wish I had notes to refer to."

"You knew Brody was engaged to someone a few years before he met Summer, right?"

"Yes. I believe her name was Elena?"

"Correct. Raven is Elena's daughter. She and Brody had grown very close, and they still keep in touch. She must be about fourteen or so by now."

The trip to the zoo was great fun, and Grace enjoyed spending time with Raven.

"Do you get to see Brody very often?" Grace asked, and Raven rolled her eyes in typical teenage fashion.

"Only when my mother decides to let me. I think she misses being linked with someone famous more than she misses Brody himself."

Brody's parents were there keeping an eye on Leo and Lucia as well as Sam and Alex, and Summer was keeping an eye on Autumn and Spencer.

"Don't they remind you of us in the beginning?" Summer asked sincerely.

"In the beginning?" Brody pretended mock horror. "Does that mean the honeymoon is over?"

"You know what I mean. Do they look like two people who are going to go their separate ways in the not-so-distant future?"

"They do not. But don't interfere. They need to figure this out for themselves." Even as Brody said the words, he knew his wife well enough to know she would not keep her opinions to herself.

After the zoo, everyone returned to Summer and Brody's house for a picnic.

Autumn complimented Summer on the spread. "So, how did you manage this? Mom and Dad and Lynn and Mitch were all with us. There's chicken and pulled pork and—oh my God! Are those biscuits from the Loveless Café?"

When she took a bite, she sighed with pleasure, and all Spencer could think was that the only other time he had seen her with her eyes closed in pure bliss was when he was making love to her.

"You have a bit of strawberry preserves right—there."

When he licked the corner of her mouth, she sighed and then she grumbled.

"Who had the bright idea of separate bedrooms?"

"You suggested it, and I agreed."

"And, by the way, why did you agree?" She sounded annoyed that he had gone along with the plan, even though it was what she had wanted at the time. And still wanted?

"Because you were right. We need to take things slow, take our time…"

"I like it when you take your time," she purred, and he almost lost his reserve.

"And I will." He tucked a stray strand of hair behind her ear. "But I want to know everything about you."

"Like what?"

"Who was your fifth-grade teacher?"

"Mr. Ferguson."

"Who was the first boy you kissed?"

"Josh Bradford."

"Who was the first man to, ah," he struggled with how to word the next question, "light your fire?"

There was no hesitation when she answered, "You."

"I'm serious."

"So am I. But let's finish that conversation when we're alone."

There were so many things she wanted to tell him about: former boyfriends, why she and Dallas were better off as friends, the kind of man she had pictured marrying someday. And while it was true that she couldn't give him children, she could still share his life, his bed, his home, and help raise his children that she had taken into her heart. And, for the first time in her life, she was allowing herself to truly open up her heart, considering possibilities she refused to consider before: a surrogate. Adoption.

Spencer wondered what the faraway look in her eyes was about, but he didn't want to break the spell.

Grace was enjoying Raven's company, and Summer decided that her sister and Spencer could use some alone time and offered to let all the kids stay overnight.

Spencer and Autumn held hands on the way home and walked silently into the house. She felt oddly nervous. She wanted to seduce him, but she did not want him to turn her down.

"Wine?" she asked." Hot tub?"

"Wine, yes. Hot tub, no. It would be too … tempting. Seeing you in those tiny things you call a bikini made my blood boil and …"

"And?"

"This." He placed her hand on his erection. "You make me feel like a teenage boy who has just discovered sex. Which reminds me – you need to explain that comment you made earlier."

"I'll be back with wine and an explanation in just a minute."

She lingered in the kitchen long enough for him to consider going to look for her when she returned with a bottle of wine and two glasses.

"You sit. I'll pour. And if you're trying to tell me I am the first man to light your fire, I'd be flattered, but a little inclined to think you were stretching the truth a bit."

"I've had sex with, well, honestly, not all that many men. Before Dallas, there was a brief flirtation in college when I was a freshman and he was a senior. I thought I was in love, but he just wanted to score with as many freshmen as he could. So, my first time was not the kind a young woman dreams about. Then there was Jay, who I started seeing sophomore year. I think I was trying to convince myself I loved these guys so I could make excuses for wanting to sleep with them. Jay ended up –"

He cut her off with a kiss. "You don't have to give me a play-by-play, nor do I want one. I just need to know, who were the important ones? After Jay, was there someone else? Or was the next someone Dallas?"

"The next someone was Dallas. I actually met his brother Devon first. They came to campus looking for men and women to appear in some of their advertisements for their sporting goods store. He singled me and a couple of other girls out and took us to meet Dallas."

Spencer's eyes darkened, wondering if it had been their intention to have Autumn pose provocatively in a swimsuit next to a boat. In his mind, she was hot enough to grace the cover of the Sports Illustrated Swimsuit Issue, but he didn't want her to think he was only interested in her body.

"So, what happened next?"

"It was a hot summer…"

Now his mind went somewhere else, and his pulse quickened.

"And?"

He had expected embarrassment but got laughter instead.

"It was something like 90 degrees outside, and I was in a room with fake snow, wearing a parka and sitting on a snowmobile. Then in February, when it was freezing outside, I was doing ads for a jet ski."

"Hartford Sporting Goods! I remember the jet ski ad."

"Be serious."

"I am serious. It made me want to buy a jet ski, and I didn't live anywhere near any water. You were wearing a black and white swimsuit that wasn't flashy, but it somehow made you look sexier than if it had been revealing."

She was amazed that he got all the details right, including the description of the swimsuit.

"You'll be happy to know I still have that swimsuit. I'd be happy to model it for you."

"You're killing me, Autumn. I'm trying really hard not to think about sex 24/7. Get back to your story before I change my mind."

"I loved Dallas, and I got engaged to Dallas, and I planned to marry Dallas until…"

"Until?"

"Until Summer and Brody fell madly in love. It was like something out of a movie. One day, I woke up and realized that Dallas was never going to look at me the way Brody looked at Summer. And while we had a very passionate and active—"

"Stop right there. I do not want to picture you with another man, even if he was your former fiancé." He did not want to think about another man making her come apart in his arms. "Was that the only reason you ended your engagement?"

She spoke so softly he almost couldn't hear her. "I didn't feel … cherished until you. You were the first man to make love to me. I knew in the beginning you didn't love me, but you made me feel like it was possible."

The final wall surrounding his heart shattered into a million pieces, and he was filled with gratitude.

Autumn continued before he could think of an appropriate response.

"So, I guess the answer you are looking for is this. Once I fell in love with you, I realized that everything I felt for every man before you paled by comparison. But look, I know you can't say the same thing about me, and that's okay. I love the fact that you were so in love with Julia. It shows me what kind of man you are, what kind of husband, what kind of father."

He was touched and humbled. "I know that love is about more than sexual compatibility, more than fireworks, more than wanting to turn you on and turn you inside out, but you are the one who ignited that flame of passion in me. Honestly, I thought I that part of my life was over. Then you kissed me, and all I could think about was what it would be like to make love to you. Slowly, completely, passionately. A first kiss had never had that effect on me before." He couldn't bring himself to come right out and say that his first kiss with Julia had not had the same effect on him, but it was true.

Autumn looked at him with tears in her eyes. "It was your last first kiss."

"And yours as well."

Right then, in that moment, Autumn knew she already knew all the important things about him. She knew that in addition to being a good listener, a good father, and an amazing lover, he was also responsible, trustworthy, warm, compassionate, and fiercely loyal. He checked all the boxes she never knew she wanted checked. She knew something had brought them together. Was it fate? Was it Julia? Was it three children who desperately needed a mother figure?

She had to admit to a certain curiosity about the women who had come before Julia, but whatever she might learn wouldn't change her mind about how she felt. Spencer was her future.

She sat her wine glass down and climbed onto his lap.

"Autumn – I thought we agreed –"

"Oh," she said while she slowly removed her top and her bra, "I still want you to take me out on dates. Take me to dinner or dancing. Go on family outings with the kids and my family. Your family." He snorted at the last one but lost all train of thought when she placed his hands on her breasts. "But …"

"But?" he drew a ragged breath and tried to ignore what her wiggling was doing to him.

"But that doesn't mean we can't also do … this." She rose up to drop her shorts and panties on the floor and guided his hand to her moist, throbbing center.

She was rewarded when he drew a finger in and out as slowly as he could, knowing it would drive them both to the edge of reason.

"We can wait," he offered, even though his body was screaming *YES* !

"I know we can wait. But why would we want to?"

"Delayed gratification? Think of the fireworks we could set off if we waited, I don't know, eight weeks?"

"Eight weeks? Are you insane?"

"Well then, how about this? Tonight, we make love all night long. And then, we wait. Eight weeks."

"Four."

"Six. And I'm firm on that."

"Oh, you're definitely firm all right." She reached down to caress him, knowing he was as close to the edge as she was. "And you have far too many clothes on."

When they satisfied their craving for each other, she looked at him and asked, "What next?"

"I need a little time to recover."

"Should I go put on the swimsuit?"

"Save it for our real honeymoon. I want to take you someplace hot and exotic because you're hot and exotic. I want to make love to you under the stars, in the ocean. I want you to crave my touch the way I crave yours."

She whispered in his ear, "I already do."

He wondered every day how it was possible that this woman was his. She was kind-hearted and sweet, but she was also saucy and sexy. She made him hard and hungry and jealous of every man who looked at her.

Chapter Seventeen

A utumn felt like her life was perfect, except for one missing piece of the puzzle. She didn't just want a baby; she wanted Spencer's baby, and she needed to find a way to make it happen.

Once school started, it became easier for her to schedule appointments with fertility specialists after school, but no one could give her the answers she wanted. The answers she needed. All she wanted was a glimmer of hope. But when she stopped to think about all the times they had already had unprotected sex, she knew she was kidding herself. If she could get pregnant, it would have happened already.

One Saturday, Spencer had a meeting, Grace was at a guitar lesson, and Sam and Alex were napping. Autumn decided to take out her frustrations on the weeds in her garden.

Autumn was knee-deep in dirt when an unfamiliar woman parked in the driveway, walked around the house, and asked in a haughty voice to see Spencer.

"He's away, on business." Autumn stood up, conscious of her scuffed, stained jeans and dirt-covered t-shirt, and decided not to offer her hand. "And you are?"

"Janet Knight. And you are – what, exactly? Gardener, housekeeper?"

So, this was the infamous Janet. Oh, how she relished the chance to put this woman in her place. But first, she wanted to have a little fun with her.

"Both," she answered, not adding that she was also Spencer's wife. "Can I offer you some coffee? Lemonade? Sweet tea?"

"I have never understood the fascination southerners have with sweet tea. But some lemonade would be lovely, thank you."

The minute Janet was inside, she asked to use the powder room, and Autumn took the opportunity to send Spencer a text that she knew would make him laugh. 'Your friend Janet is here,' she typed. 'It's obvious from the looks she was giving me that she thinks I'm beneath you.' His immediate reply made her laugh and blush. 'I love it when you're beneath me. Keep her entertained. I'll be home soon.'

Janet returned, and Autumn handed her a frosty glass of lemonade. "The twins are asleep. I brought the monitor inside, but we could sit on the porch if you prefer."

"The twins are still here?" Janet asked in an incredulous voice.

"Where else would they be?"

"Oh," she hastily tried to backpedal, "I just thought … never mind."

Autumn suddenly wondered if Janet and Laura were, or had been, in on the plan to take custody of the twins away from Spencer. This was an unexpected turn of events.

"Are you in town for business?"

"I'm a financial advisor."

"Oh, so Spencer is a client?"

Janet frowned at Autumn's casual use of Spencer's first name.

"No, we're friends. Close, personal friends," she replied with an emphasis on the word 'personal.'

They exchanged a little more impersonal chit-chat when Janet said, "Don't let me keep you from any of your, ah, duties."

"Oh, it's fine. I was almost done weeding, and the twins should be awake any minute. They are such lovely, sweet girls. Did you ever meet them?"

Janet tried unsuccessfully to repress a shudder. "Toddlers can be so – demanding."

"So, no children of your own?"

"Not yet. But, you see, Spencer and I used to be romantically involved and - "

Whatever Janet was about to say was cut off by Spencer's arrival. He burst into the room, saying, "Darling! I've missed you!"

Janet preened and stood, expecting an embrace, pleased he was so pleased to see her. So, it took her by complete surprise when he not only hugged Autumn but kissed her in a way he had never kissed Janet.

"I'm sorry my conference lasted longer than I expected. How are you and my girls?"

Janet cleared her throat, and he turned as though noticing her for the first time.

"Janet, what a - surprise." The fact that he did not refer to it as a nice surprise did not go by unnoticed. "I see you and my wife, Autumn, are getting to know one another. The girls and I are crazy about her."

The sour expression on Janet's face made it appear like she was sucking on a lemon. "And how long have you and Autumn been married?"

Spencer shrugged and said, "Who needs to count when every day feels like we are still on our honeymoon?"

If anything, the look on Janet's face got darker.

"And here I thought she was the housekeeper."

Autumn didn't feel inclined to trade barbs with her and sink to her level.

Spencer laughed. "She does it all. I don't know where she gets the time or the energy because she certainly doesn't get much sleep at night." He winked roguishly at his wife.

"I can't believe a woman in this day and age settles for being a housewife." Janet said it like it was a dirty word.

"Oh, I'm not. I teach third grade. I help build houses for Habitat for Humanity. Volunteer once a month at the local animal shelter and," she lowered her voice as though she was about to divulge a secret, "every once in a while, I get to work backstage at an arena show for Martin Brody."

That got Janet's attention, and Autumn was not surprised. Her brother-in-law was hugely successful and had been voted Music City's Most Eligible Bachelor before he fell head over heels in love with her sister.

"Martin Brody. Seriously?" The look on Janet's face was both envious and disbelieving.

"All true," Spencer backed her statement up. "He is my biggest client, and that's actually how I met Autumn. He's married to her twin sister, Summer."

"That explains a lot."

"And what is that supposed to mean?" Spencer was tired of playing nice. He couldn't believe he hadn't seen behind her mask sooner than he had.

"You have twins; she has a twin. It's easy to connect the dots. I wasn't ready to play step-mommy, so you found someone who was. But I have to say, I am surprised Laura fell for this charade. Why, the last time we talked, she acted like getting custody of Sam and Alex was practically a done deal." Janet turned pale, suddenly realizing she had said too much.

Spencer advanced until he was inches away from her face. "Let's just get a few things straight before I show you to the door. First of all, for the life of me, I have no idea what I ever saw in you. You are a hard, unfeeling woman, and Autumn is the complete opposite. She's warm and kind and treats my children as if they were her own. I was smitten after our first kiss, and I never looked back. You can run to Laura and tell her I was mean to you, but go take a good, long look in the mirror first. You are a conniving, cold-hearted bitch. Autumn doesn't just warm my bed; she also warms my heart."

"You men are all alike. You might pretend you want a nice, normal, stable woman like me when what you really want is a sexpot."

"I'll take the sexpot comment as a compliment since no one has ever called me that before," Autumn said with a deceptively sweet smile.

"You were a swimsuit model," Spencer reminded her as Janet turned even greener with jealousy.

"True. And I will also thank you, Janet, for giving us some insight into Laura's motives. Why, you might have turned the tide in our favor. But now I want you to get the hell out of my house!"

Autumn's eyes were flashing fire, and Spencer had never seen her that angry before.

"Time to leave, Janet," Spencer echoed.

Janet had to have the last word. "Mark my words, you will be sorry about the choices you have made."

The minute she was out the door, Spencer and Autumn looked at each other and said in unison, "Janet and Laura?"

"Janet never seemed comfortable around Sam and Alex, but I just chalked it up to them going through a difficult time and her not having children of her own. But now I wonder who planted the first seed."

Fortunately, Sam and Alex didn't wake up until Janet was gone, and Autumn announced that it was time for milk and cookies.

Spencer watched as his two bright, beautiful girls took Autumn's hands to follow her into the kitchen. As soon as he smelled freshly baked cookies, he followed close behind them.

"Daddy wants cookies too," he said as he snatched one off a tray. "Oatmeal raisin, my favorite. When did you have time to bake homemade cookies?"

She handed him the empty Pillsbury package still sitting on the counter. "Not exactly homemade. All you need to do is put the little individually pre-made squares on a cookie sheet, and voila! But I am going to ask Grace for more cooking lessons. It seems ridiculous that your twelve-year-old is a better cook than I am."

"I don't care if you can't turn on the stove," he whispered in her ear, "since you can definitely turn up the heat in the bedroom."

Before Autumn could think of a suitable answer to say in front of Sam and Alex, they went off, milk and cookies in hand, to play in the family room.

"Sadly, not for another four weeks and six days."

"You know, we haven't talked about what's going to happen when the four weeks and six days are up."

"I'm thinking a weekend away at a romantic B&B," Autumn suggested.

"And I'm thinking about a remote cabin far, far away from everything and everyone where we can make as much noise as we want to. You do love to scream out my name when I—"

"Stop talking about it!" Autumn exclaimed, wondering how she was ever going to keep her hands off him. He was not the only one who thought about sex 24/7.

The following Wednesday, Summer and Brody agreed to watch the kids so Spencer could take Autumn out on a proper date.

He picked her up at school and got to meet a few of her co-workers that hadn't been able to make it to the party. He thought one of the fourth-grade teachers looked more than a little disappointed that Autumn was unavailable.

When she slid into the car next to him, he pulled her in for a long, lingering kiss.

"I saw the way Mr. Preston was looking at you."

"Tyler? You're kidding, right?"

"Men notice those things. He was looking at me like he hoped I would just disappear."

"Just because you want to have hot, wild sex with me doesn't mean every other man does."

"Trust me. Unless they are happily married, over 80, or gay, they do."

She pretended to consider that. "Hmmm. So maybe all those guys that came after Dallas wanted me and not an introduction to my famous brother-in-law after all."

"Or maybe they wanted both. Fortunately for me, none of them got close enough to you to light your fire."

"Don't let it go to your head."

"Too late."

She looked out the car window and suddenly realized she had no idea where they were.

"Where are we going?"

"It's a surprise."

"Is it a remote cabin where you can make me come with your hands and your mouth and your incredibly hard—"

"Stop. Talking. Now."

She glanced down to see the effect her words had on him and smiled to herself as she wondered if the magic would last forever.

"Can you give me a hint?"

"What is it about the word 'surprise' that you don't understand?"

Soon he pulled up to a lovely piece of land and got out a blanket and a picnic basket.

Autumn found it enchanting. "How romantic!" She clapped her hands as he brought out wine and cheese and fruit and crusty French bread. "But where are we? Who owns this land? We don't want to get caught trespassing. Especially if we get naked."

He gave her a stern look. "We are not getting naked. As for the land, it's for sale. Brody knows the owner and he hinted to him that my wife and I might be interested in buying it so we could build our dream home here."

Autumn had no idea he was thinking along those lines. Even though he and Julia had never lived together in the current house, there were times when Autumn felt like the interloper. It just didn't feel like 'their' home, but she couldn't quite put her finger on why.

She finally found her voice. "And are we? Interested?"

"We can have that discussion in a little less than four weeks. But this is only the beginning of our date. After our picnic, I have another surprise planned."

To say she was surprised when they pulled up in front of a dance studio would have been an understatement.

"Seriously? I mean, I'm game, but I will probably embarrass us both in front of the other students."

"There won't be any other students. I signed us up for two lessons a week for the next three weeks. When we're done, we might be able to waltz."

"You are way more optimistic than I am. I hope you still love me when I step all over your feet."

The instructor was a forty-something-year-old woman who assured Autumn that she had taught students of all ages and abilities during her 15-plus years as a dance instructor.

"I'm Saundra, and I look forward to learning more about you and why you have come to my studio."

"I have two left feet," Autumn admitted.

"So, do we want to learn a dance for a special event? Are you planning a wedding?"

Autumn opened her mouth to say they were already married when Spencer made a statement that rendered her speechless for the second time that evening.

"We are. You see, the first time we had a private civil ceremony, but this woman deserves a wedding with all the pomp and circumstance: the wedding gown, the cake, the reception, a bridal dance, and, most especially, a second honeymoon."

Autumn was even more surprised by this than she was when he suggested building their dream house together. She assumed Spencer and Julia had had a wedding with all the trimmings. She wanted to say something in response, but words failed her. How was it possible that she had captured the heart of this sentimental, thoughtful man? She finally understood Summer comparing Brody to a magical unicorn – a man too good to be true.

Chapter Eighteen

They were taking turns planning their dates, and her turn was next. She was having a hard time coming up with an idea when Grace suggested cooking lessons.

Cooking lessons had never crossed Autumn's mind, although she readily admitted she needed a lot of help in the kitchen. She discovered an advertisement for a creative cooking class at the local community center, and signed them up for the entire eight-week class, even though that extended past their self-imposed deadline.

The night of their first cooking class, she arranged to pick him up at work. He had been spending more and more time there recently, along with Brody, as they were in the middle of negotiations with a potential new client Brody wanted to sign to his record label.

When she went looking for him in his office, the sight that greeted her made her quickly move to the side of his office door out of sight. A blonde, long-legged beauty seemed practically glued to her husband. Her first reaction was to either confront them or run, but she instead hung around to see what happened next. While their marriage had not started out as a "real" one, it seemed to be becoming more like one every day.

"What are you doing?" she heard Spencer ask the woman in an angry voice.

"If you have to ask, I'm not doing it right."

"Serena, zip your dress back up. I'm a married man. A happily married man I might add. When I said we should celebrate you signing your contract, this was not what I meant."

"No one has to know we had a little fling. But somehow I don't think little is a very accurate description."

"My wife is going to be coming any minute now."

"You could be too. And there'll be no need for messy condoms."

Autumn wanted to gag. How could anyone be so brazen? She risked a quick peek inside and saw Spencer pick something up on his desk before she moved back into the shadows.

"See this? Your contract signed by everyone but Brody not more than 10 minutes ago? Which, by the way, he said he would be here to sign."

"I told him not to come. I know women fall at his feet, but I like the strong, silent type more than someone with his blatant sexuality. So, he can sign it tomorrow. In the meantime, since your wife is on her way, let's celebrate alone later. I'm in the penthouse suite at the Omni downtown."

"I am not going to come to your hotel room," Spencer said in a firm, no-nonsense voice.

Serena refused to take no for an answer. "Well, if you're afraid someone will see us together, and word would get back to your wife, my limo driver could bring you to my hotel."

"Let me make this perfectly clear. I am not going anywhere with you. Not only that, I'm done with you. We are all done with you and I can tell you right now it's a damn good thing Brody didn't sign this contract, because he does not want someone like you on his record label."

"What are you doing?" Serena's voice rose an octave, and Autumn peeked in just in time to see Spencer ripping her contract to shreds and throwing it up in the air like confetti.

"I told you I'm done with you. The minute Brody puts the word out about you, no one will sign you. My advice is to go back to LA, because as soon as you are on that plane, no one in Nashville will remember your name."

"Then I'll tell Brody that you were the one that came on to me, tried to seduce me, wouldn't take no for an answer."

"Good luck with that, honey," Autumn said as she entered the office. "Because I heard every word."

Serena shrugged her off as inconsequential and didn't back down.

"And just who do you think is going to believe you?"

Autumn started counting on her fingers. "Number one, Spencer, my husband. Number two, Summer Martin, Brody's wife. Who, by the way, also happens to be my sister. Your days are numbered in this town, so take my husband's advice and get out of here and don't look back."

Serena seemed unwilling to admit defeat, but the look in Autumn's eyes changed her mind and she made a quick exit.

An uncomfortable silence stretched before them after Serena made her departure. Autumn seriously wondered what transpired before she arrived. But, she didn't ask.

"Will Brody really blackball her?"

"In a heartbeat. Admittedly, I think he heard something in her voice that I didn't. To me, she leaned a little more towards a pop-country sound, and I didn't think she would be a good fit for the label."

"She's definitely attractive enough. All that long, wavy, blonde hair and those big—"

"I'm pretty sure hers are not real." The words were out of his mouth before he realized what it implied.

"And how would you know?" Autumn was getting steamed and beginning to wonder if her imminent arrival had made a difference.

He threw his hands up in surrender. "It was just an observation! I have no first-hand knowledge, trust me. You have to believe me when I say I was never tempted. Not even for a minute."

"Well, you aren't getting any at home."

"You are the only woman I want in my bed."

"Then prove it to me."

A kiss was not exactly what she had in mind, but his tongue captured hers in a dance, and she felt like melting into his arms. But before she could stroke him to the point of no return, he took a step back.

"I know what you're thinking," he said with a smoky look of desire.

"What do you think I'm thinking?"

"You want to lock the office door and shove all the papers off my desk so you can drive us both over the edge."

"Hmmm. You're right. That was what I was thinking."

"Then think about how hot the sex is going to be after our trial period is over."

"Is that how you're looking at it – like a trial period?"

"I know that's not a very apt description. We both agreed we did everything backwards. We got married, fell

173

into bed, and didn't think very long and hard about the consequences."

"Serena was right about one thing when she was imagining that it was long and hard. Because I love it when it's long and hard and driving me over the edge."

"You are a foxy little temptress. But before you talk me out of my clothes, which I admit would not be all that difficult to do, why don't you tell me what you have planned for tonight?"

"We're going to be cooking."

That conjured up all sorts of images. "In the …?"

"Now *you* need to get your mind out of the bedroom. We're taking cooking classes. Your daughter informed me that we need to expand our repertoire."

"Some things do get better with practice," he reminded her.

Much like the dance lessons, they enjoyed the cooking class, and meeting some of the other couples in the class. She hadn't really thought about the fact that pretty much all their social interactions involved family or co-workers.

They held hands, talking and laughing the whole way home.

"I hadn't really thought about it before tonight," Spencer said, "but being part of a couple is spending time with other couples, having outside interests. I know you have your co-workers, and I have mine, but it might be a good idea to make some new friends."

She wasn't surprised that his comments so mirrored her own thoughts, as it seemed they were starting to have similar opinions about any number of things. But in the next breath, she thought, what if we don't stay together? He keeps his kids, but who gets the friends?

"Earth to Autumn. What's on your mind?"

Rather than say what was on her mind and ruin the moment, she went for sarcasm instead.

"I'm all for making new friends as long as one of them doesn't have to be Janet. I mean, seriously, I can't figure out what you saw in the woman."

He spoke so softly she had to strain to hear him.

"She was safe."

They stayed up late into the night, talking about their future, making plans, and trying to convince each other that someday soon Grant and Laura would back off.

The following weekend, Spencer had a meeting scheduled with Brody and a new act he wanted to sign. He had agreed to let Grant and Laura see Sam and Alex, and Autumn offered to take them to Grant and Laura's house.

"The deal was that they would come here," he reminded her.

"I know, but a college friend of mine lives not far from them, and it would give me a good chance to see her. I told Sharon we would stop by after the twins' visit is over."

Laura seemed calmer and more rational than Autumn had ever seen her, and she secretly wondered if Janet had gotten in touch with Laura and told her to back off a little.

When Autumn was getting ready to leave, Laura informed her that she had a box for Grace.

"Her mother's jewelry box is in there. Spencer has Julia's valuable jewelry to pass along to all the children when they are older, but I gave Julia a locket when she turned 13, and we would like Grace to have it on her 13th birthday. We know we won't be seeing her on her actual birthday, but we want her to know we are thinking of her."

If this was an act, it was working. Somehow, Laura had accomplished the impossible and made Autumn feel sorry for her.

They left to visit Autumn's friend Sharon and her two young boys, who were close in age to Sam and Alex. They all scampered off to play, and Sharon breathed a sigh of relief.

"Paul and Kevin can be so rambunctious. Having two children under the age of four is a daily struggle. I'm not quite sure how I am going to manage with three."

"You're pregnant again?"

Sharon nodded. "Mark's mother took the boys for a night a couple of months back, and we celebrated a little too much. Next thing I knew, baby number three was on the way. I swear all he has to do is look at me and I get pregnant. I just hope this one is a girl. I told Mark three was my limit."

Autumn was green with envy. She would give anything to be pregnant with Spencer's baby, boy or girl.

Even though she enjoyed catching up with Sharon, she left feeling out of sorts. She was also dreading the day when Summer announced she was expecting again. When Summer had gotten pregnant with Leo and Lucia, Autumn had not felt one bit envious, nor had she felt the loss of Evie then as keenly as she did now.

When they arrived home, Sam and Alex were both half-asleep in their car seats, and Autumn hoped they would nap once they were in their own beds. By the time she got them both settled down, she had completely forgotten about the box for Grace.

The dancing and cooking lessons were going well. As they started to make some new friends, Autumn felt cautious but also optimistic. Ben and Nicole and Steve and Jennifer didn't know their story or their background, and it made Autumn feel like she was living a lie. But she did not voice that to Spencer.

As their self-imposed deadline grew closer, Autumn started to get nervous. They didn't have many disagreements and no real fights, and she sometimes wondered if they were trying too hard to be perfect instead of just being themselves.

One Saturday morning, the twins both woke up on the wrong side of the bed. Grace was at a sleepover, and Spencer was on a conference call in his home office.

"We want Mickey pancakes!" both Sam and Alex were demanding in loud voices.

"Today we're having waffles with strawberries and—"

The twins were normally well-behaved for their age and not known for interruptions and outbursts, so their attitudes took Autumn by complete surprise.

"Mommy always made us pancakes," Sam announced.

"That's right, and you're not our Mommy." Alex stuck her tongue out at Autumn.

Autumn took a deep breath and counted to ten. When she announced that she was not making pancakes, their voices rose to a level that reached Spencer's attention.

He took one look at Autumn's face and the identical storms brewing in the faces of his youngest children and asked, "Does someone want to let me know what all the screaming is about?"

Sam responded by pointing to Autumn and saying, "She won't make us pancakes, and she's not our Mommy."

Alex started to cry and say that they wanted their "real" Mommy.

For the first time since Spencer and Autumn had gotten married, he was truly torn between wanting to comfort his children and scold them at the same time. He knew in his heart that this was an important moment and that Autumn would be paying careful attention to how he'd respond. In the end, he pulled up a chair and sat between Sam and Alex.

"It's not nice to be mean to Autumn, and it's also not the way you normally treat her." He knew this was about far more than pancakes, but he was at a loss as to what it could be about.

"Did something happen the last time you saw Grandma and Grandpa? Did they say mean things about Autumn or tell you she did not deserve to be treated with love and respect?"

"They gave something to her and she hid it from us!" Sam exclaimed.

For the first time since leaving Grant and Laura's house, Autumn remembered the box for Grace.

"Oh, girls, I feel awful. Laura did give me a box, but it's not for you. Your Grandma gave me a jewelry box to give Grace on her next birthday. It's still in my car."

"A jewelry box?" Spencer questioned.

"It belonged to Julia, and there's a locket in it that they gave her on her thirteenth birthday. They want Grace to have it."

"Girls," Spencer said in a stern tone he seldom needed to use with the twins, "you need to apologize to Autumn. She always treats you with kindness and she loves you."

To their credit, the twins did not hesitate to reach out to hug Autumn and say in tandem, tear-filled voices that they were sorry.

The matter was resolved, but not entirely to Autumn's satisfaction. She wanted to chastise Spencer for not pointing out that while she was, in fact, not their "real" mother, she was their mother in all the ways that mattered. Unless he didn't see it that way.

Chapter Nineteen

T he following night, there was an intense, violent storm with hurricane warnings. The house had a room in the basement with no windows and enough provisions to get them through a night or two at most. Autumn was more nervous than the rest of them put together, pacing back and forth and running her fingers through her hair.

"Have you experienced a hurricane and the destruction it can leave in its path?" Spencer asked, thinking it was the only thing that made any sense.

She simply answered that she had not, not wanting to add that the only thing she had had worth saving had been lost in a move.

Spencer thought she seemed more agitated than he had ever seen her before.

"What's bothering you?"

"I don't like storms." She continued to pace around the room. She felt claustrophobic even though the room was not that small. They had brought down candles, flashlights, and sleeping bags. The twins started giggling and carrying on about having a slumber party, but Autumn knew sleep would not come easy for her.

"It sounds like the wind is already starting to die down. I really don't think there is anything to worry about," Spencer said as he tried to reassure her.

"What would you do if you woke up and it was all gone? There must be something you'd be heartsick to lose. Maybe something of a more sentimental than valuable item?"

"All the things that matter most to me are right here in this room." He raised her left hand to his lips and kissed her wedding ring. "And that includes you. But what about you? Any family heirlooms?"

"I lost the only thing that mattered to me a long time ago." She wiped away a stray tear and changed the subject, realizing that the girls were picking up on her anxiety. "Let's read the Magical Unicorn books."

In the morning, all was right with the world, but Autumn still felt unsettled. She felt like the storm continued to rage on the inside. It brought up longings and memories she thought she had left in the past.

The following day, Autumn got an unexpected text from Dallas that simply said, "Call me. It's important."

Both surprised and curious, she called him back immediately.

"Hey, stranger. What's up?"

"First of all, congratulations, I heard you got married."

"Thanks, and I heard your wife is expecting. You'll be a great father, but somehow I don't think you called me just to catch up."

"Gina and I just moved. Crazy, I know, since she's pregnant. But I found something when I was unpacking. I found Evie's ring."

Her heart stopped. The one possession she prized above all else.

"Will you send it to me? Overnight it to me so it doesn't get lost?" She thought it was gone forever and couldn't bear the thought of losing it a second time.

"I can do one better. We're opening a store in Franklin, and I'm here this afternoon. Why don't we meet somewhere so I can give it to you in person?"

She was so rattled that she forgot about Grace's guitar lesson. They had hired a nanny when Autumn went back to school, and when Autumn didn't show up, Laurel drove Grace to Brody's house and called to let Spencer know Autumn hadn't called or shown up.

The first thought that crossed his mind was to wonder where had she run off to this time with no word to anyone. The last time it happened, he had found her at the coffee shop, so he decided to start there, even though it seemed more likely that she had gotten held up at school. So, he was taken aback to see her there, this time sitting with a different man.

He was proud of himself for not immediately jumping to conclusions. He reminded himself that this could be anyone —someone else from the support group, a new teacher, or an old friend.

He had his hand on the door, about to go in, when he stopped in his tracks. To his shock and dismay, he saw his wife slip off both her engagement and wedding rings, and the man placed a different ring on her finger. She was smiling and crying simultaneously when she got up and wrapped the other man in a lengthy embrace.

Spencer walked back to his car in a fog, barely able to comprehend what he had just witnessed. He wanted to confront them and stay hidden at the same time. Unsure of what to do, he decided to wait in his car to see how long they would stay at the coffee shop, if they would leave hand in hand, or exchange a passionate kiss. He remembered what she had said about a last first kiss. She had said it with such heartfelt conviction that he had believed it, believed her. Had she meant it at the time, or had she just said what she thought he wanted to hear?

Even though he wanted answers, he also did not want to confront her with anger and suspicion like the last time. He decided to plan a romantic dinner for two, call Summer or Kelly to see if they could watch the kids so he could wine, dine, and seduce his wife. They were down to the last few days, so what difference could it make if they didn't wait to rekindle their passion? To fan the flames back into a forest fire?

Decision made, he signaled to pull out of his parking spot when his wife and the mystery man exited the coffee shop. He held his breath, waiting to see what happened next. He almost leapt out of his car when they embraced, but the man merely kissed Autumn on the cheek. Autumn walked in the direction of where he assumed her car was, and the man watched her walk away.

Spencer wished he could get a better look at the expression on the other man's face. Would it be longing? Regert? Desire? All the things he felt when he looked at Autumn?

The man hesitated before getting in his car, and the sunlight caught the glint of his wedding band. Spencer couldn't decide if he was relieved or angry that the guy was married. Did that make the situation better or worse?

Spencer did some errands before he got home and called Summer and Kelly, but they both had plans for the evening. A romantic evening for two wasn't in the cards.

As he pulled into the driveway, he wondered what her mood was going to be like. Happy? Sad? Distant? Itching for a fight so she could turn the tables on him? Goad him into overreacting so she could feel justified in leaving? Then he realized her car wasn't there.

As dinnertime approached and she still wasn't home, he began to worry. Then she called to say she had stopped at Summer's house. She apologized for missing Grace's guitar lesson but made no mention of where she had been earlier.

When she finally got home that night, it had gotten late. All the children were already in bed, and he wondered if she had planned it that way.

As relieved as he was to see her walk in the door wearing her engagement and wedding rings, he had learned his lesson after her last coffee shop date. He refused to jump down her throat, demand an explanation, or ask who she had been with. Instead, they had a polite, although strained, conversation, and they both went to bed, alone.

The following night was their final dance class. While Autumn expressed that she was fine, Spencer knew her well enough to know that something was simmering just below the surface, and he kicked himself for not trying to have a discussion the night before. He planned to ask questions in a non-confrontational manner and, more importantly, listen.

The instructor asked if they were interested in signing up for a couples' dance class beginning in about six weeks, and Autumn declined politely before they even had a chance to discuss it. While it was true that he wasn't sure he would have wanted to continue, he had to ask himself why she wasn't even willing to consider it or ask for his opinion.

On the way home, he asked if she wanted to stop for a glass of wine or a cup of her favorite frothy beverage, hoping she might choose to go to her favorite coffee shop. If this new man happened to be there, what would she do? Avoid him and pretend she didn't know him? Introduce him?

In the end, it didn't matter because all she wanted to do was go home.

Kelly had stayed with the kids. Sam and Alex were already in bed. Since Kelly and Grace had a close relationship, Autumn and Spencer were surprised she and Grace weren't sitting on the couch watching a romantic comedy.

"She's on the phone," Kelly said with a smile. "With a boy."

"A boy?" Spencer raised both his voice and his eyebrows.

"Is it Ian?" Autumn inquired hopefully.

"Ian? Who's Ian?" Spencer demanded rather than asked.

"A boy in her class. She's hoping he will ask her to the 8th-grade dance."

"Did you tell my twelve-year-old daughter she could date?" The topic had never been discussed in his presence, and he was both shocked and thoroughly annoyed. "Julia would never approve of this."

Kelly shot him a warning look, but he ignored her and kept digging a deeper hole.

"It's not your place to make decisions like that. I'm her father."

"I'm well aware of that," Autumn snapped. "And no, I did not tell YOUR daughter she could date at 12 or 15 or 23. She mentioned that there was a boy in her class she liked named Ian. There. Now you know as much as I do." She stalked off down the hall towards her bedroom, anger coming off her in waves.

As soon as she was out of sight, Kelly punched Spencer in the arm.

"Are you trying to alienate her?"

Spencer looked oblivious. "What?"

"What? Seriously?" Kelly did a perfect job of imitating his voice when she said 'did you tell my twelve-year-old daughter she could date?'"

"It's not like Autumn is her mother."

"You are a colossal idiot. She may not be their biological mother, but the last time I checked, she's the closest thing Grace has to a mother. But if you don't get your act together, you might be raising your three daughters all by yourself. And after what I just witnessed, if that does happen, you will have no one to blame but yourself. And I'll tell you one more thing you are not going to like. If you don't make things right with her, and she leaves, you will never again find a woman with such an open heart."

Autumn had only ventured far enough down the hallway to eavesdrop on their conversation. She appreciated Kelly sticking up for her but felt sorely disappointed in Spencer. She, of course, had no intentions of interfering with his parenting rules or final decisions. But how could she be an integral part of their family if he wanted to exclude her from that? And the thing that hurt the most was that he brought Julia up. Was Autumn forever to live in her shadow? Never measure up?

She heard Kelly leave but was in no mood to speak with Spencer. Her feelings were raw, and her heart was hurting. She couldn't do anything more than give him her all, and if that wasn't enough, if she wasn't enough, it was time to say goodbye. She just couldn't bring herself to do it quite yet.

She had a meeting at school first thing the next morning and turned in early. When Spencer approached her door to try to make things right, he could tell there were no lights on, and he vowed to talk to her first thing in the morning.

But when morning came, Autumn left earlier than she needed to, having given up on getting a good night's sleep at about 5:00 am. Since Laurel could get Grace on the bus and the twins off to preschool, she saw no reason to wait around.

Spencer, however, was surprised to find Laurel there fixing breakfast, and he found it unnerving that she seemed so at home in his kitchen.

He managed to choke down a few pieces of French toast soaked in maple syrup that tasted like sandpaper. When he remarked that he was surprised Autumn hadn't fixed breakfast, Laurel reminded him that Autumn left for an early meeting at school.

He did not voice his suspicions aloud but half wondered if she really had an early meeting or if she was off meeting her mystery man. Should he drive by the coffee shop on the way to work?

Once Grace got on the bus and Laurel and the twins were out the door, Spencer did something he swore he would never do. He searched Autumn's room looking for the ring the other man had given her. He checked the ceramic bowl on the dresser that held several bracelets, but no ring.

He even went so far as to search her bathroom, looking in her tampon box to no avail. He returned to her bedroom and continued his search. But he didn't realize Laurel had returned and saw him.

His day at work went from bad to worse, and he found it nearly impossible to concentrate. Was Autumn truly in love and committed to him, or just a really good actress? Their chemistry was undeniable, and it pained him to admit to himself that while he and Julia had loved one another unconditionally, they didn't have that raw sexual energy. Their marriage had not been perfect, no one's was. But now that Autumn shared his life and his bed, took Grace and Sam and Alex into her heart, he wondered if she was the one. The missing piece of the puzzle, the person to complete him. But he wasn't sure if it was real for her.

Chapter Twenty

Across town, Autumn kept changing her mind about what to say and do. Had the time come to face the fact that life with Spencer would never be what she wanted it to be? Needed it to be? His comments about "his" daughter wounded her, but it went deeper than that. Spencer didn't seem to realize how his words affected her. She found it hard to believe that that one moment made her question everything, but it did.

If she had known Spencer was feeling the same way, she would have rushed to his side to tell him about meeting Dallas so he could return Evie's ring.

As the evening before their self-imposed deadline date drew near, Autumn struggled with the war between her head and her heart. She thought about asking Summer for advice but wasn't sure how much to share. She would have loved to confide in Kelly, but it wasn't fair to put her in the middle, even though Kelly never hesitated to speak her mind, or tell Spencer what she thought about his words or actions.

Spencer invited Autumn to a special announcement at Brody's record label, but she had no interest in going, especially since Spencer had been going on and on at length about this new artist, how talented she was, how everyone was looking forward to working with her.

Spencer didn't understand why she didn't want to go, but neither did he question her about it. And somehow, that just annoyed her more. Surely the incident with Serena should have taught him something?

Instead, she stayed home to work on her birthday gift for Grace and also to make sure the jewelry box and locket were in good condition and needed no repairs.

The box was lovely, obviously handmade, and the locket beautiful. Nothing needed to be refinished. She was surprised, however, to discover an envelope addressed to Spencer in the box. If it had been sealed, she would not have opened it, but the back flap was open, and curiosity got the better of her.

She expected a love letter, or perhaps a letter Julia had written after her diagnosis, so Grace would have something from her to read on her thirteenth birthday. But what she discovered was so unexpected that it took a moment for her to process what she was reading. It was a birth certificate and an adoption certificate. Julia Marie Montgomery had been adopted by Grant and Laura. She was not their biological daughter.

This changed everything. Autumn sat for a long time, thinking about the repercussions. Obviously, Spencer was completely unaware, which begged the question – why did Julia never tell him? If nothing else, at least from the standpoint of her medical history.

She knew she needed to tell Spencer, show it to Spencer, but by the time he got home that night, it was close to midnight, and she decided that tomorrow morning was soon enough.

It did not escape her notice that tomorrow their trial period, as he once called it, was over. While on one hand the news that Julia was adopted was a game changer, but it was not likely to set a romantic mood.

She and Spencer had both taken the day off and had given Laurel the day off as well. Summer offered to take Sam and Alex to preschool, pick them back up, and keep them for a sleepover. Grace was going home after school with a friend for a slumber party. Everything had been planned for a perfect romantic day and night alone.

As soon as Autumn came into the kitchen for breakfast, Spencer picked up on her mood, but when he asked her what was wrong, she just shook her head and said they would talk about it after everyone left for school.

Once the children were all gone, Spencer fully expected Autumn to make a provocative suggestion, but all she did was stand there looking like she had lost her best friend.

"Autumn, I -"

"Spencer, I -"

"Ladies first."

"I found out something last night that is just.... well, unbelievable."

If she had said it in an elated voice rather than a sad one, he would have guessed that against all odds she was pregnant. But he could tell from the look on her face and her voice inflection that that was not it.

"You're scaring me. Are you okay? You're not sick, are you?" He shuddered at the thought that he could lose another wife to a terrible disease.

"Yes. But here – just read this. I found it in the jewelry box. If the envelope had been sealed, I never would have opened it. I don't want you to think I would ever invade your privacy." Now he felt even more guilty about searching her room.

"Just be prepared," Autumn continued. "Maybe you want to sit down."

What, he wondered, could possibly be that important? Life changing?

He removed the two pieces of paper, and she could tell the minute he realized the significance of what he read.

He fell into the nearest chair, stunned beyond belief.

"I never had any idea. Not an inkling. Why didn't she tell me?"

She could also tell the minute his expression turned from confused to upset.

"What if one of the kids inherited some genetic disorder?" He paused to take a deep breath and try to regain some sense of balance. "I wonder if I ever really knew my wife at all. What else did she keep from me?"

"Spencer, I know you are reeling from this unexpected news. For right now, just concentrate on what this means in terms of the custody battle. Grant and Laura aren't related to Sam and Alex by blood. I realize they have always been present in their lives, and some sympathetic judge might grant them visitation, but not full custody. You need to go call your attorney right now and let him know."

"You're right."

Autumn left to give him some privacy and to go slip into some new lingerie.

Before Spencer could say more than hello, Luke announced that he had news.

"So do I. You go first."

"Laura's attorneys are fighting hard for a DNA test. I feel like you need to agree so it doesn't look like you are trying to hide something. I know you have been dead set against it, but I think that you need to -"

Spencer interrupted him before he could finish. "Set it up."

"What?"

"Set it up. I will agree to it, but only on one condition."

"What's that?"

"Laura and Grant need to agree to get tested as well."

"Where is that coming from?"

"I just found out, literally seconds ago, that Julia was adopted. Grant and Laura aren't her biological parents, or, obviously, Sam and Alex's biological grandparents. But the icing on the cake is that they don't know that I know."

"A surprise attack. They won't see it coming. I like that. But I have to ask, what does this mean for you and Autumn?"

"First of all, I cannot believe Julia never told me. And if I had known this, I could have saved everyone a lot of heartache. I wouldn't have married Autumn. I never planned to get married again after I lost Julia. I never wanted to get married again."

Spencer had not heard Autumn's silent approach, and she stopped dead in her tracks. She could barely breathe. In that moment, the only thought running through her head was that if she hadn't given him the adoption certificate they would be celebrating right now. He would be making love to her; they would be talking about the future. Their future. Assuming they were talking at all. But instead, her heart was breaking into a million little pieces.. He didn't need her anymore. Wanted her in his bed, that was undeniable. Their chemistry was off the charts, but she knew that wasn't enough. And she also knew she could not live her life in Julia's shadow. To have her every comment or suggestion turned into 'Julia would never …' The issue of Grace dating made that glaringly obvious.

But she told herself to wait, to see what he said next. To give him the benefit of the doubt. After all, she had misinterpreted his conversation with Laura because she hadn't stuck around to hear the entire conversation.

If Luke responded, she missed it. The next thing she heard Spencer say was that he was going to go talk to his wife. She waited for him in their bedroom, but the next thing she knew, she heard him driving away in his car. So, where was he going?

She walked around nervously for a few minutes and picked up the birth and adoption certificates to read them again. And then it hit her, the thing that she had not noticed and he had not mentioned. Today was Julia's birthday. Suddenly, she knew exactly where he had gone. To the cemetery. To talk to his wife.

She didn't leave immediately because she wanted to observe him from a distance, far enough away that he wouldn't notice her but hopefully close enough to hear what he was saying. They had taken the children there on the anniversary of her death, so she knew the location of the cemetery and her grave.

She arrived to find his car parked on the side of the driveway near her grave and approached silently. His shoulders shook and he was so overcome with emotion he could hardly speak. It seemed obvious he was feeling a flood of different emotions - anger, disbelief, and grief.

"I thought you and I shared everything. I thought I knew all your secrets, your hopes, your dreams, your disappointments. We buried our son, and before I could deal with that loss, I lost you. The love of my life. The woman I wanted to grow old with, watch our children grow up." He started to sob, and Autumn was torn between wanting to comfort him and wanting to leave to let him grieve in private. She knew logically that the only reason she was with him was because Julia was not, but hadn't they started to build something together? Not a traditional family, but a family nonetheless?

His next words shattered her already bruised heart. "How can you ever, ever forgive me for what I've done? I thought I was doing what you would have wanted me to do. We never talked about how you wanted me to go on after your death. It was like if we avoided the subject, you would magically recover. This life I am leading is not what ... "He was struggling, and Autumn decided she had heard enough. "It's not what – it's not what I wanted."

She turned around abruptly, almost tripping over a branch on the ground, and raced to her car. She left to go to their house, no, she corrected herself, his house.

Spencer suddenly felt Autumn's presence but when he turned around she was already gone.

He stood and said, "I don't know if you can understand all the reasons I married Autumn. The life I have with her was not what I wanted in the beginning. In the beginning, I did it for our children. To keep my family, our family, together. But I never expected to fall in love with her. I never expected to feel all the emotions I never thought I would feel

again, and some I had never felt before. It sounds dishonest
to your memory, I know. But if the situations were reversed, I
would have wanted you to find love again, to go on living,
and not stay stuck in the past. Your parents don't understand,
nor do they want to. You will always live in my heart and my
memories, but my heart belongs to another now, completely
and without reservation. It is long past time I told her that.
She took your children into her heart, and she loves me and
the three of them unconditionally. She ... saved us."

Chapter Twenty-One

I nstead of going right home, Spencer stopped and bought a bottle of her favorite wine and her favorite flowers. He was mentally preparing for all the things he needed to say. What to say to make her understand his heart now and forever belonged to only her.

When he arrived home, he couldn't believe his eyes, stunned to see the guest room in a state of disarray. Suitcases half-filled, clothes in a heap on every available surface, and most disheartening of all, her engagement and wedding rings on top of the dresser.

Did this mean since he didn't need her anymore that she didn't need him anymore? Did she not love him? Want him? Want to stay married for the right reasons?

He walked down the hall to hear her talking softly on her phone, and all his questions were answered. They just weren't the answers he wanted to hear.

"I know I told you Spencer would need to keep up this charade of a marriage for a couple more years, but I learned something – well, more than one thing today – that changed everything. I know I made you a promise before I met Spencer and I'm calling to say that I am ready to fulfill it now. I know neither one of us is getting any younger, so we shouldn't wait any longer. I've decided to give you the child you want."

He heard laughter and a few tears, but he was rendered speechless.

"Dani, I'm ready to do this. Make plans for the future. Your future, our future."

He could only conclude that she was talking to the man in the coffee shop, the one who placed a different ring on her finger. If that wasn't devastating enough, it also led him to believe that the whole 'I can't have children thing' was an elaborate hoax. If she simply didn't want children because he had three of his own, or even if she was worried about having another miscarriage, he could have understood. They could have talked through it, worked through it. But he had to face the fact that it wasn't that she didn't want to have children; she didn't want to have children with him.

"I'll need to work through the divorce details with Spencer, but I can be there soon. I see no need to wait."

So much for a last first kiss, he thought. Not that he could imagine ever wanting to kiss anyone besides Autumn. In a way, this loss cut deeper than the loss of his first wife, the mother of his children. Julia may have left him, but she had not chosen to leave.

If Autumn had just come to him, wanting to leave because the whole reason they had gotten married didn't matter anymore, he would have been devastated, but he would have wished her well. But this, this was different. Heartbreaking. Gut-wrenching. His children loved her, and he knew without a doubt that she loved them. But had she ever loved him?

He was heartsick. He had given his heart again, only to have his worst fears come true.

He locked himself in his office until bedtime, hoping against hope that she would come looking for him and offer an explanation. Brutal honesty would have been better than deceit.

They both spent the night alone in their respective bedrooms, each nursing a broken heart because they were too afraid to face one another, each believing that the person they loved wanted out.

At least twice, Spencer approached her room and stopped himself before knocking and begging her to stay.

The following morning, Spencer went to work, absolutely certain she would not leave without some sort of goodbye, even if it only a phone call. Hell, he'd even settle for a text.

After a restless night's sleep, Autumn continued to go over everything she had heard again, even though the words were burned into her brain. She simply went through the motions.

Spencer was gone before she got up, and she called in sick. Fortunately, none of the children were there to witness her abject misery.

Autumn was about to call Spencer when Laurel showed up, having forgotten that she did not need to take Sam and Alex to preschool that day. Autumn tried to send her on her way, but there seemed to be something on Laurel's mind.

"Mrs. Sullivan..." she hesitated before continuing.

"I've told you a hundred times you can call me Autumn."

"This is difficult for me."

And there it was, Autumn thought hopefully. Laurel was going to give her notice. And Autumn would have an excuse to stay a little longer with the man she loved. Even if he didn't love her.

"I saw your husband searching your room a few days ago. He doesn't know I saw him, so please don't say anything. But I thought you should know."

Autumn knew she might be making it up to cause trouble, but her struggle seemed genuine. And, at this point, what did it really matter?

Once Laurel left, Autumn saw no point in trying to have a reasonable conversation with Spencer, especially now that she knew he had been searching her room. For what? Signs of an affair? Love letters written to or from another man? His jealousy was unfounded, but he jumped to conclusions about any relationship she had, however innocent, with another man.

In the end, she decided on a letter instead of a phone call. She knew if she heard Spencer's voice she would fall apart. She would explain about Dani. How could he fault her for wanting to be a surrogate for her dearest friend? Autumn knew if she ever decided she wanted to be a mother, that Dani would not hesitate to do the same for her.

She started the letter at least a dozen times until finally deciding to write to Grace first. Sam and Alex were too young, and as the years passed, would likely not even remember the woman who had been a part of their lives for such a short time.

The tears were flowing when she finished the letters and placed them on their pillows.

When she walked out the door for the last time, she turned around and saw their future without her. She wouldn't be there when Grace became a teenager, learned to drive, went on her first date. Wipe her tears from her first heartbreak. She wouldn't get to watch the twins grow up and form their own individual personalities, like the same boy, and make new friends. Her heart was hurting, and hurting for so many reasons. She was just a short chapter in the lives of Spencer and his children. Would Sam and Alex even remember her?

In that moment of perfect clarity, she realized that the three of them had taken over the empty spot in her heart left behind by Evie. She had always thought about, wondered about, what Evie would look like. Would she have resembled Dallas? Would she have drawn Autumn and Dallas closer together? She didn't regret Dallas, but neither did she miss him terribly when they parted. Spencer was another matter entirely. She knew she would miss him until her dying day.

As she drove off, she knew she would have to call her sister sooner or later, but she opted for later since she had absolutely no idea what she was going to say.

It didn't take her long to get to Dani and Drew's house, which was close to her school and had a mother-in-law apartment attached to their spacious home with its own separate entrance. They had tried for years to have a baby without success. They had bought the house with the idea of having separate but close accommodations for a live-in nanny.

Dani wasn't exactly a household name, but she had a recurring role on a nighttime soap opera and recently auditioned for a small role in a movie. If she got the role, it would require relocating to California for the duration of filming. Autumn hoped she would get the part so she could put some miles between her and Spencer.

Dani and Drew were thrilled to see her and gave her some privacy to settle in. As she unpacked, she was both hoping for and dreading a call from Spencer at the same time.

When Spencer got home to discover her gone and the guest bedroom empty, he was hurt but not entirely surprised. But what did surprise him was that there was no note, no words of goodbye. No explanation.

What neither he nor Grace knew was that Sam and Alex had found the letters and hid them in what they called their "treasure box." Along with a picture of their mother, it held assorted odds and ends.

When Grace asked her father where Autumn was, she was met with a stony glare and a few clipped words. All he said was that she had left them. Spencer knew Grace would not be content for more than 24 hours at most with his brief explanation, so he went to Summer and Brody's house hoping to see Autumn or at least find out where she was. He was upset that she had not said goodbye to him, but livid that she had not seen fit to say goodbye to Grace. She had promised she would always be a part of Grace's life, even once no longer married to Spencer. Was that just another empty promise?

As soon as Summer asked why Autumn had not come along with him, he knew they knew nothing about what had transpired. And he refused to be the one to fill them in.

Every morning when he woke up, he thought about driving by the school, and every morning he talked himself out of it and just headed to work.

Laurel started pitching in to do more, started staying later, cooking dinner, and trying to subtly insert herself into every aspect of their everyday lives.

One night, after Sam and Alex were tucked in bed, Grace informed her father they had a serious matter to discuss.

"Laurel needs to go. I've been looking online for her replacement, and I found a few possibilities."

"What are you talking about?"

Grace rolled her eyes. "Dad, seriously? You haven't noticed the way she looks at you or the way she started dressing? Nicer clothes? More makeup?"

He looked at her blankly. If Laurel had been trying to make him interested in her, he had missed the signs.

"She wants to take Autumn's place."

"Not in a million years. So, show me what you found."

A week later, Laurel was dismissed and a grandmotherly type, Maureen, stepped in. The twins took to her immediately, and Spencer was greatly relieved Grace had been able to see through to Laurel's true motives.

One day, Spencer decided he needed to find out something, so he went to the person he expected would have the most up-to-date information.

"Do you want to come in for a cup of coffee?" Brody asked.

"I need something stronger. Whiskey?"

Spencer started to open up, while having no idea what Brody knew or didn't know.

"I don't know what to think. Was any of it real? It was real to me, but I always felt like she was keeping secrets from me. I just never dreamed that the secret would be another man."

Summer stormed into the kitchen like a hurricane. "You are an idiot who doesn't know the first thing about my sister or the truth or love. If Brody wants to continue to have you represent him, that's his business. But let me make myself perfectly clear. I never want to see you again. You are not welcome in this house."

"Summer, I just don't understand—"

"No. Just no. I regret the day you came into our lives. Into my sister's life."

She walked away, and Brody didn't know quite what to say, so Spencer let him off the hook.

"It's okay, Brody. I'll talk to Evan about someone else in the firm taking over for me. The last thing I ever want to do is cause trouble for you and Summer."

Chapter Twenty-Two

TWELVE MONTHS LATER

Autumn held her divorce papers in one hand and the results of the last round of in vitro in the other. She was waiting for Dani and Drew before opening either one.

A few minutes later, Dani burst into the house on cloud nine. "I got the part! California, here we come! This is a much more significant role than the last two I auditioned for. Drew – go get the champagne so we can celebrate!"

"Let's hold off on that for a moment, shall we?" Autumn held up her left hand. "Divorce papers." Then she held up her right hand. "Lab results."

Dani sank onto the nearest chair. "It would be too much to hope for two pieces of good news in the same day." She realized how that sounded and immediately apologized to Autumn. "Autumn, I'm so sorry. I meant about getting the part – not about - "

"No need to apologize. I knew the divorce papers were coming. I hoped, dreamed, that Spencer would change his mind. But if he can't understand what I wanted to do for you, then, honestly, I'm better off without him."

Even though she had known the papers were coming, it was difficult to stop the tears from flowing.

She handed the envelope containing the lab results to Drew. "Why don't you open them?"

She knew if the results were negative again, even winning the part would not make this any easier for Dani.

When Drew opened the envelope, he sank down in the chair next to his wife. "It's positive! We're going to have a baby!"

Dani jumped up and wrapped her arms around Autumn, who was crying now for a different reason. She was thrilled for Dani and Drew, thrilled that she could make their dreams come true. But she was also overcome with sadness that she would never feel Spencer's baby grow beneath her heart.

"How can we ever thank you?" Drew asked.

"By being wonderful parents."

"There are no words," Dani said. "We can never repay you for the sacrifice you have made for our family."

Autumn had also made a sacrifice for Spencer, but in the end it mattered little. So, the next day, she signed the divorce papers. She had already resigned from her teaching position. It had become too difficult to walk into school every day and wonder if this was going to be the day when Spencer showed up to declare that he still loved her.

She didn't know what she would do once the filming was over and the baby was born. She couldn't imagine being very far away from her family permanently, but she also did not want to risk running into Spencer, especially if he had another woman on his arm.

Once, she came close to asking Summer what she knew about Spencer, but Summer shut down the question before Autumn could finish. Autumn tried to tell herself she was better off not knowing. But the not knowing was killing her.

When Spencer received the signed divorce papers, he wanted to rip them up, pretend they were still married, pretend she was still his wife and not about to become someone else's since she was now free to remarry. It was obvious she had moved on without so much as a backward glance, but the same could not be said of Spencer. He still missed her every day, with every fiber of his being. Grace had turned into a moody, uncooperative teenager who kept asking her father what he had done to drive Autumn away. He had no answers.

SIX MONTHS LATER

The filming of the time travel movie was wrapping up, and Autumn was relieved. She couldn't help but think about how she wanted to travel back in time. But even knowing how it had all turned out, she knew she would never have been able to forgive herself if she had kept the information about Julia's adoption a secret from Spencer. The pregnancy was making her tired, and she was also tired of all the commotion. There were reporters on the set daily, trying to wrangle interviews with the big stars.

One night, Spencer and Grace were watching some Hollywood entertainment-type show that he loathed but Grace loved when suddenly, there she was. She was standing next to a handsome man on one side and a glamorous, beautiful woman on the other, but he only had eyes for his wife. Because in his heart, she was still his wife. He knew he would never, could never, give his heart to another.

Daniella, known to her friends as Dani, used her middle name as her stage name. Her agent had insisted that no one would ever be able to spell her first name correctly, so everyone knew her as Marie London.

Grace was the first to speak. "I can't believe she's there with Marie London! I wonder if Autumn has a part in the movie."

Spencer was tempted to remark that she was a good enough actress to be in a movie, but he couldn't stand to look at Autumn another minute. He reached for the remote control when Grace's next words cut him like a knife.

"Dad – is she pregnant?"

Not only was she pregnant, she was glowing. And he could only assume that the man on the other side of her was the man she had left him for.

Images of Autumn began to haunt his days and his nights again. Some nights he would wake up dreaming her hands or her mouth were wrapped around him, and he would be hard and depressed.

He somehow managed to avoid Summer for months, but she too was pregnant, and he ran into Brody from time to time at the office. While he was genuinely happy for them, at the same time he wanted to wipe all thoughts of pregnant women and babies from his mind. He knew he needed to look for another job, a new job where no one knew about his late wife, or his second wife who ran off with another man before their divorce was even final.

He received a job offer from New York and another in Miami, but he didn't want to uproot his children. He did decide they needed to move to another house—one half-built that someone had begun and ran out of money before finishing. He needed to be somewhere where images of Autumn weren't around every corner. They mocked him at every turn: the hot tub, his home office where one day he had indeed let her sweep everything off his desk so he could pleasure her. The images of making love to her were burned into his brain, but at least a new house would have fewer memories.

Autumn had returned from California to await the birth of the baby and to attend the wedding of her brother, Carter. While part of Autumn hoped she would run into Spencer, part of her was afraid—afraid she would throw herself into his arms and plead for an explanation as to why he had just cut her out of his life. But she was even more afraid she would see him with a woman, looking content and happy. Happier than he had obviously been with her. She knew it was past time to accept the fact that she had simply been the means to an end. The only way for him to keep Julia's precious children with him.

One day, a few weeks after seeing her on television, Spencer drove by her favorite coffee house only to see a familiar car. He might not have recognized it without the vanity plates, but he was sure the car belonged to her mystery man—who, he assumed, was Danny.

He went in on a whim, not knowing what, if anything, he would say.

He had only seen the man briefly before, but there was no doubt it was him, because a pregnant Autumn was sitting next to him, holding a child that looked to be a few years old.

The moment Autumn spotted him, he swore time stood still. Should he greet her? Turn around and leave? Slug the guy?

Just then, another woman joined them and took the child in her arms. The man put his arm around the back of her chair. Things just got more interesting, Spencer thought.

"Hello, Spencer." Autumn managed to get the words out somehow, even though seeing him both excited and depressed her equally.

He greeted her, then extended his hand to the man. "Spencer Sullivan."

The man's eyes turned as dark as midnight. If he was staking his claim, who was the woman and child?

"Dallas Hartford," he answered in a harsh but firmly controlled voice. "This is my wife, Gina, and our daughter, Iris. We already know who you are, so don't bother sitting down."

Iris started to fuss, and Gina left to change her. Spencer was relieved he could ask just one question without Gina overhearing.

"Not planning to sit down. If you could indulge me by answering just one question, Autumn."

He could tell that took Autumn by surprise, but all she said was, "I can't promise to answer, but go ahead."

"What did he give you the last time you were here?"

Autumn looked completely confused. "What?"

"I watched him take off your engagement and wedding rings and put a different ring on your finger."

She had no idea he had seen them because he had never mentioned it.

She stood and held up her hand, shaking with emotion and anger. Naturally, he had assumed the worst. Wasn't that what he always did? Question her loyalty when he had been the one in the end to say he wouldn't have married her if he had known Julia was adopted?

She held her hand up. "Is this the ring?"

"I don't know. Is it?"

"This is the ring Dallas gave me when we lost Evie. The ring I thought had been lost years ago. He found it when he and Gina were moving, and he brought it to me. He knew how much it meant to me, and I would have been happy to explain that to you if you had only asked. But no, you jumped to conclusions just like you always did."

Any second now, her emotions and hormones were going to get the best of her, and she was going to lose it. She just couldn't do it in front of Spencer.

Spencer simply said, "I'm sorry," and turned to walk out of the coffee shop.

Autumn regained a small measure of control. He had almost made it to his car when she came out after him.

"Is the ring what you were looking for when you searched my room?"

Now it was his turn to look confused. "What?"

"Don't bother denying it. Laurel told me all about it."

He couldn't deny her accusation, but she was a fine one to talk.

"You have no right to fling accusations at me while you are standing here pregnant. I don't think I ever knew you at all. And stop texting my daughter. She's gotten as good as you at keeping secrets, but that stops now."

Autumn couldn't believe what she was hearing. How could he possibly be upset about her being pregnant? She had laid it all out in the letter to him.

She returned to Dani and Drew's house upset and angry. She was glad they were still in California for a few more weeks because she didn't want to talk to anyone.

Spencer was 100 times more upset and took it out on Grace the minute he walked in the door and saw her on the phone. He grabbed it out of her hands to make sure she wasn't talking to Autumn.

"It's Becca! What is wrong with you?"

"You are never to communicate with Autumn again, do you hear me? No calls, no e-mails, no texting. Nothing. You do not understand what kind of person she is."

"No!" Grace shouted. "It's you who doesn't understand. She loved me. She loved you. She loved all of us. You did something to drive her away, and I hate you. If I knew where she was, I would go and live with her!"

The twins could hear their father and Grace arguing, and it scared them. They had been too young when Autumn left to understand the consequences of taking the letters. They were still hidden in their treasure box, completely forgotten.

A few months later, both Summer and Autumn went into labor. They had joked about giving birth on the same day since their due dates were only a few weeks apart, but Autumn was still surprised when Dani and Drew's son decided to come early.

Both babies were born shortly before midnight. Leo and Lucia had a new brother, Christopher, and Dani and Drew also had a son, Carson.

Spencer didn't know that Autumn had given birth when he swung by the hospital to congratulate Brody and get a peek at the baby in the nursery.

He didn't get to see Brody, but he went to the nursery anyway. He half-expected to see reporters converging on the hospital, but news of the birth of Brody's newest child was still under wraps.

There were, however, two nurses hovering by the nursery window that obviously knew who Christopher's famous father was.

"He's as handsome as his father," one of them sighed.

"He has his eyes."

To Spencer, Christopher just looked like a newborn. But something about the baby on the left caught his eye.

"And look at little Carson," the first nurse said. "What are the chances that twin sisters would give birth at the same hospital on the same night?"

Spencer felt all the air leave his lungs. So, Carson was Autumn's son. A feeling of grief so intense washed over him that one of the nurses turned and asked if he was all right. He murmured a few words and left before he could come face to face with the man who had fathered Carson.

For the next few days, he walked around in a daze, caught between being happy that Autumn's dream of becoming a mother had come true and crushed that he was not Carson's father. It would have mattered little to him if the baby had been a girl. It was not about a replacement for Ben. It was about wanting to have a child with the woman who had brought him back to life.

Chapter Twenty-Three

Their new house was not due to be completed for several more months, but Spencer suddenly found himself wanting to change everything or nothing in their current house. But he knew nothing would drive the memory of Autumn from his heart.

He and Grace finally reached an uneasy truce, and one day he asked if she would like the mural recreated in her bedroom at the new house.

"I knew I forbade you to contact Autumn, but I could reach out to the art teachers at her school."

"Don't bother." He could tell Grace was struggling with trying to keep her emotions in check. "She left me. Left us. And besides, I'm too old." Autumn leaving affected Grace in much the same way losing her mother had. But she kept her feelings to herself.

Summer was still writing the Magical Unicorn books, and Sam and Alex were still fascinated with them. One night, when Grace was at a sleepover, Spencer sat down and asked the girls if they wanted to have the characters from the books painted in their room at the new house. He knew for him it would be one more reminder, but they did love them.

"We each want our own rooms. We're big girls now," Sam announced, and her sister nodded her head in agreement.

He thought about all the time Autumn had missed. Before he knew it, she would have been gone for two years. And yet, the hole in his heart was just as big, if not bigger. Seeing her son had gutted him.

When he stood up to lean against the bookshelf to wipe away a stray tear before either of the girls saw it, the treasure box slid off and landed on the floor, the contents strewn about.

"I'm sorry, girls. I -" he stopped and stared at two envelopes with familiar handwriting. One was addressed to him, and one to Grace. They were wrinkled but unopened. In a voice he barely recognized as his own he asked, "Where did you get these?"

"From Mommy Autumn."

"When?"

They both shrugged, not able to verbalize how much time had passed. Finally, Alex said, "It was a long time ago, when you were really sad."

He was still sad; he just tried harder not to show it.

"Girls, it's time for bed. When you wake up in the morning, we can talk more about you each wanting your own room."

But, of course, bedtime never went that smoothly or that quickly. They wanted a story, a glass of water, to pick out different pajamas. His babies were growing up, and even though he treasured every moment with them, tonight all he wanted was to be alone to read the letter. He had waited so long for an explanation, never dreaming he would actually get one. Or get one that made sense.

As soon as he opened the letter addressed to him, he was not at all surprised to discover she wrote it on the day she left. He began reading with shaky hands and what felt a lot like a glimmer of hope.

"My dearest Spencer," it began, "You and your children were my whole world, my heart, and you were the love of my life. My world ended when I heard you tell Luke that if you had known Julia was adopted, you would not have had to marry me. And then you went to the cemetery and begged Julia to forgive you for marrying me. I knew we had jumped in too fast, had not considered the consequences, but I thought all that had changed. I thought that no matter how our marriage started out, it had become real to both of us. I knew in the beginning that I was just a means to an end. And I accepted that. But then I fell in love with you. I know the passion came first, the heat, the all-encompassing need. But every time you made love to me I fell a little bit more under your spell. I wanted more than anything for us to be a family. But when I realized that we were never going to be the kind of family I wanted, I needed, I made the decision to give my best friend the family she wanted and needed. Dani, Daniella Marie London, has been my best friend (don't tell Summer I said that) since the third grade. And much like me, she and her husband Drew cannot have a baby without medical intervention."

He had to stop reading to wipe the tears away before he could continue.

"I hope someday in the future you will understand and forgive my hasty departure from your life. Some exes can be friends. I guess I consider Dallas to be a friend. I was never his one and only, and he was never mine. I didn't find that out until I found you. You were mine for a while, and I will never forget you. I hope that Grant and Laura back off now, because I could never have left if I thought you still needed me."

It was true that Grant and Laura had backed off as soon as he demanded they submit to a DNA test. And much to his surprise, their relationship improved after that, and they spent a lot of time with not just the twins, but with Spencer and Grace as well. Still, that took nothing away from the fact that Autumn had stepped in when he needed her.

His mind flooded with memories of dance classes, cooking classes, hearing her read to the twins, tucking them in, singing silly songs at bath time, encouraging Grace to open up more, and encouraging him to open up more. But he knew if he wanted to win her back, he needed a plan, and a lot of help.

He sent Grace a text to let her know everything was okay, but that he would appreciate it if Becca's parents could bring her home. Next, he called Kelly and told her he needed some love advice. She knew he was still in love with Autumn, so she hurried over, arriving at the same time as Grace.

"Do you have any idea what this is about?" Grace asked and Kelly shook her head.

They walked in and looked at him expectantly, and he blurted out, "I'm an idiot."

Neither responded immediately, but by the look on their faces, he could tell they both agreed.

He took out Autumn's letter and began to read it out loud. By the time he was done, he was not the only one crying.

Grace hugged him and said, "Bring her home," and went to her room to read her letter.

The wheels were starting to turn in Kelly's head. "Spencer, this will require a grand gesture on your part. Is she the type to want your reunion to be a private one? Just you two? You and the kids? You and her family?"

Before he could come up with an answer, Grace came running down the stairs, looking happier than she had been for a long time. "Dad, I know what to do."

Phase one of the plan was set into motion the following week. Even though Spencer wanted to run to her, sweep her up in his arms, and swear his undying love, he knew it needed to be bigger than that.

One day shortly after he and Autumn got married, Brody shared with him the story of a brief misunderstanding that he and Summer had before they were married. How he thought all hope was lost until he saw her standing before him during the filming of the music video for Summer Love. Spencer wanted it to be as big, or bigger, than that. A moment Autumn would never forget. A moment the two of them would cherish for the rest of their lives.

Summer was doing a very limited book signing at a local bookstore and not doing a full-fledged book tour since Christopher was still so young.

Kelly took Alex, Sam, and Grace to the bookstore, which was limited to 20 customers. They timed it so they could be the last ones in line.

Grace was still taking music lessons from Brody, although she had mastered the guitar and moved on to the keyboard. So, when she handed Summer a note to pass along to Brody, Summer assumed it was related to her music lessons. Brody was busy recording a new album and had not seen Grace for the past three weeks.

Fortunately for Spencer, Brody was 100% on board with Spencer and Grace's idea and promised not to share the news with anyone, including Summer.

They had two more weeks to finalize the plan. Brody was going to be appearing at the Bridgestone Arena with several of the new artists he recently signed to his label. Somehow, he managed to convince Summer's entire family, including Autumn, that this was a must-see performance.

The arena had sold out, and Summer and her family occupied most of the front row. Spencer and Grace stayed out of sight backstage.

Both of the new acts were greeted enthusiastically by the crowd, but they were all on their feet, chanting and screaming the minute Brody took the stage.

He sang a few of his well-known hits before he made an announcement.

"It's been a closely guarded secret that I am working on a new release. I had just about finished recording when I realized it was missing something very important: a very special love song for a very special woman."

Autumn grasped her sister's hand and said, "I always love the love songs he writes for you."

But when Brody started to sing, it was not a love song to or for Summer. It was, instead, a song called "Falling for Autumn," and only the people in the front row understood the significance of the title.

When the song was over, Brody invited the two people who co-wrote the song to join him on stage, and Grace and Spencer walked out.

When Spencer began to talk, Autumn could not contain her emotions, and the tears started falling unchecked down her cheeks. He talked about losing his first wife to cancer, his second wife to pride and jealousy, and a failure to communicate. He finished by saying, "I stand before all 19, 950 of you tonight to ask for Autumn's hand in marriage."

Grace motioned for Alex and Sam to join them on the stage. "And we stand before all 19, 950 of you tonight asking Autumn to be our mother."

No one, least of all Autumn, had seen this coming. Summer was equally surprised and thrilled. And she couldn't believe Brody had managed to keep it a secret.

Autumn raced up on stage and could only nod her head to accept their proposals, her heart beating a mile a minute as if it was going to burst.

"I take it that's a yes?" Spencer asked, and the crowd erupted.

Later, Brody pointed out that not many people got a standing ovation following a marriage proposal.

There were long talks into the night about the parts of the conversations Autumn and Spencer had both overheard. And while they were both understandably upset with the twins and what they would come to refer to as the "lost years," they knew all that mattered was that they were together now, stronger than ever. They knew in their hearts the bond would never again be broken.

Brody used his private plane to fly both families to the Grand Hotel so Autumn could have the same kind of fairy-tale wedding her sister had had. Autumn thought their lives were complete until they flew home and Spencer said he had one more surprise for her.

He drove them around in circles for a while until she started to alternately laugh and pepper him with questions." Where are you taking me?"

"We're almost there. Close your eyes."

For once she did as she was told and could not believe it when he told her she could open them. There standing before her was a half-finished house situated on the same lot where they had gone on a picnic before their first dance lesson. Spencer explained that the exterior was complete, but the interior still needed work.

"It's our dream home," she whispered, thinking about the nights they had laid awake in bed, talking about it, making plans for the yard and the kitchen and the master bedroom suite.

"It will be. It still needs a lot of work."

"When did you start to build it?"

"Actually, someone else started to build it and ran out of money. I didn't even know at first that the lot had been sold. I took over the construction. When we were separated, I couldn't stay in the house we had shared. I saw you in every corner. I thought about the mornings when I joined you in the shower and we were both almost late to work. I thought about the time in my office when you let me worship you with my mouth. I saw the murals you did for my girls."

"Our girls," she corrected him.

"And then there was the bedroom where we first made love. You set my world on fire."

"You are going to take me on a proper honeymoon this time, aren't you?"

"As long as you remember to bring the swimsuit from the sporting goods ad."

They went on a two-week whirlwind honeymoon. Brody lent them his plane and pilot. Every few days they picked a new destination, places neither of them had ever been before.

Construction on the new house was nearing completion. They both longed to make one of the bedrooms into a nursery, but Autumn thought it would be too sad if there was never a baby to fill it. They ended up leaving the room painted a neutral color so it could become whatever they wanted it to be when they moved in. They were considering turning it into a music room for Grace.

As the first anniversary of what they referred to as their real wedding approached, Summer gently broke the news to her sister that she and Brody were expecting again.

For a week following Summer's announcement, Autumn was an emotional wreck. She wasn't sleeping, wasn't eating, and was trying to spend some time with Dani and Carson before Dani left to film a new movie where she had gotten the leading role.

On the eve of their first anniversary, Autumn told Spencer she planned a special evening and that all the kids were spending the night with Kelly.

They hadn't moved into the new house yet, but it was close to being done. She cooked them a gourmet meal, and afterwards, Spencer expected her to lead him to the master suite where they could spend their first night there alone.

Instead, she took his hand and led him to the empty room. The door was closed, and she said, "I've decided what we should do with it."

His curiosity was aroused, but he suspected she had asked for Brody's input into turning it into a music room for Grace. He could not have been more wrong.

She threw open the door to a room filled with pink and blue balloons and a crib.

"Did the adoption agency come through this quickly? Do we know if it's a boy or a girl? Not that I care. I'm guessing we are getting a baby since there's a crib."

"We aren't getting a boy or a girl."

"Twins?" His eyes widened in surprise. "But there's only one crib."

"We're not getting a baby." She placed his hand on her stomach and said the words so softly he thought he must be dreaming. "We're not adopting a baby, Spencer. We're having a baby."

Just shy of eight months later, the same two nurses Spencer had seen admiring Christopher and Carson were admiring Jane and Margaret.

"I can't believe it," one of the nurses said." They did it again."

A Note From The Author

Thank you for reading my book! If you enjoyed it, I'd be incredibly grateful if you could take a moment to leave a review wherever you purchased it.

Reviews are the lifeblood of an author's career. They help new readers discover my work, influence visibility on online platforms, and directly impact my ability to continue writing books like this one. Even a brief, honest review makes an enormous difference.

Your words matter more than you know, and I read every single review with gratitude.

Happy reading,

Joan

About The Author

Joan Wahl grew up in Western New York, minutes away from the world-famous Chautauqua Institution, where she has attended lectures, concerts, operas and the ballet. She attended Mercyhurst College in Erie, Pennsylvania, although as a teenager she had unrealistic dreams of attending Julliard and studying piano.

Joan loves to travel and her favorite destinations are Nashville, Tennessee, her "happy place", the rugged coast of Maine and New York City at Christmastime. She loves to browse in bookstores and libraries, visit museums, tour historic homes, and get lost trying to locate a remote lighthouse.

Joan has been fortunate to meet many of her favorite authors, including Clive Cussler, although the list of those she would like to meet grows longer with every book she reads. Someday she hopes to be able to travel to Colorado to tour the Cussler Museum and see some of the automobiles he featured in his books.

Joan has one adult daughter and one grandson, who lights up her life with his smile.

When Joan is not writing or reading, she is having monster truck races with her grandson or cheering for her favorite football team, the Buffalo Bills.

Her husband of seventeen years makes every day seem like a honeymoon, so it seemed very natural to pen a love story.

"My musical background and love of travel converged in Nashville where I was inspired to visit iconic locations and

set my romances in Music City. My stories are warm, inviting and offer the perfect setting for fans of contemporary romance. Escape with Summer and Brody and follow along as other characters have the chance to find their happily ever after as the series continues."

Joan is the author of the **Music City series** . Find **Summer Love in Music City** and **Falling for Autumn** in your favorite book, Ebook, and audiobook stores.

Follow Joan online at http://joanwahlauthor.com/

www.ingramcontent.com/pod-product-compliance
Lightning Source LLC
Chambersburg PA
CBHW070838030726
47504CB00005B/1141